Better Together
The Cedarville Series #4
By
Bree Kraemer

Better Together

The Cedarville Series #4
Bree Kraemer
Published by Bree Kraemer, 2020.

This is a work of fiction. Similarities to real people, places, or events are entirely coincidental.
Better Together

First edition. March 28, 2020.

Also by Bree Kraemer

The Only Series
Only By His Touch
Only With Trust
If Only
Only You
Only For Love
Cedarville Novels
An Unexpected Home
Capturing Us
Choosing You
Better Together
A Chance Worth Taking
Forever Starts Here (Novella)
After All These Years
Won't Let You Down
Say When
Something To Lose
Finally Home
Friends & Brothers
Sky High Love
Bridge To Love
When It's Love
Rockstar Romance
The Right Note
Pick Me
Christmas Novella
Light Me Up
DecorHATE for the Holidays
Falling Over You
The Beckmeyer Family
Hooked
Sparked
Shocked
Kneaded
Valley Falls Strikers
Late Tackle
First Touch

Chapter 1

He pushed the last box of his stuff into the back of the moving truck and pulled the door down. This was it. He was really picking up his life and moving to Cedarville. He wasn't sure what he was expected or supposed to feel at a time like this but euphoria was the only actual thing he felt.

He, Ryan Ball, who had never done a spontaneous thing in his thirty years of living, had two weeks ago made the biggest decision of his life. A decision that hadn't felt like a decision at all.

Six months ago, he'd found out that his younger brother, Rob, and his wife, Tina, had been in a car accident. Rob hadn't fared well and died immediately, but Tina had lived a few more months hooked up to machines. The kicker was that they'd had a child, Reed, and someone needed to take care of him.

Ryan stepped up.

At least as much as he could. At the time, he'd been working sixty to seventy hour weeks, barely having time to sleep, let alone take care of a six-year-old child. So, he trekked to Cedarville for the very first time with the intention of pleading with Carly Graham to help him out.

There was just one problem: Carly had been his brother's girlfriend during college. That is until she walked in on him with another woman. The woman...her own mom, Tina. From that day forward, she hadn't spoken to her mom or Rob. Ryan hadn't had any communication with his brother either once he'd gotten together with Tina. Between the drugs and the constant calls for money, it had been too much to take.

But a child needed him and there was no way Ryan could have stood by and let him go into foster care. Not while he could do something about it.

And, thank God, Carly had seen it the same way. She'd stepped up and offered any and all help she could give, and honestly, Ryan didn't know what he would have done without her.

There had just been one big issue. Carly lived in Cedarville, Ohio, and he lived in Baltimore, Maryland. Five hundred miles apart wasn't conducive to shared parenting. But they'd made a plan. Carly would keep Reed for a month while he got organized at work so he could cut back hours. Then Reed would come back and live with him in Baltimore, Carly would visit, and vice versa.

The plan had a fault though. No one imagined that Reed – or Ryan – would fall in love with the small lake town of Cedarville. Or that Carly would fall in love with Tony and Reed would in turn fall head over heels for him. Leaving Cedarville was just not an option, it seemed. And, after a month of hating his job and missing Reed, Ryan was on board for a change.

His life had not been as fantastic as everyone had thought, anyway.

Yes, he had a great job as a tax attorney in Baltimore. And yes, he lived right in the middle of town where there was tons to do. Ironically though, he had no time to do any of the cool things because he worked so much. So, there he was a thirty-year-old man with no social life to speak of, no dates and no fun. All he had was work.

Fantastic, his ass.

He'd been ready for a change only he hadn't known it. But Reed coming into his life had forced him into the realization that he needed more. Hell, he wanted more.

So there he sat, on the bumper of the truck he'd rented, which now held all his belongings.

He was moving to Cedarville.

Letting out a breath, he stood and walked back up to his now empty condo. He'd promised Carly and Reed that he would call before he hit the road, and since there was nothing else keeping him there, he figured he'd just go ahead and leave.

Grabbing his phone, he pulled up his FaceTime App and clicked on Carly's number. It rang only once before her face popped up.

"Hey," she said, peppier than anyone had the right to be at seven in the morning. He could tell by what was behind her that she was sitting at the counter in her kitchen. "Please tell me you aren't already packed up and on the road?"

"Not on the road yet, but the truck is all packed."

"Jesus, Ryan. What'd you do, get up at two in the morning?"

He laughed. "For your information, I rented the truck last night and hired movers to help me load all the heavy stuff. All I had to do this morning was load a few boxes."

Tony's face came on the screen. "Ignore her. She's just excited for you to be moving here."

"I'm excited too." He walked around the place one last time as they talked. "I just wanted to let you know that I am headed out and, with any luck and no traffic, I should be there by three."

"We'll be here with beer, food, and lots of manly men to help you unload."

"About that," he said. "Are you sure you want me living with you?" When he'd made his decision to move to Cedarville, Carly being Carly, had offered for him to stay there. Reed already had a room at her house so it had just made sense. But, the more he thought about it, the more he wondered if he shouldn't get a place of his own.

"I told you, Ryan, Reed and I want you here. So, do me a favor, at least for now, stay here. If in the future you want to move or find your own place, that'll be cool with me."

He nodded at the phone. "All right then, I guess I'll see you later." He hit the end button and glanced around one last time before walking out the door.

There was nothing more for him there. It was time to move onward and upward.

The first half of his drive went smoothly. It was the second half where he began to question himself. He didn't even have a job lined up in Cedarville. Yes, he had worked hard since graduating law school five years ago, and, because of that and the lack of a social life, he had saved a lot of money. Not to mention – and this was crazy – his brother had taken out a life insurance policy on himself. So, when both he and his wife had died, Ryan had been able to file for it. He wasn't planning on touching that money though. He would invest it for Reed's future.

Being a tax attorney was all he knew and he doubted they had any need for that in a town like Cedarville. But, he thought he might study up on family law before taking the Ohio bar and go that route.

He laughed out loud at his predicament. In the past, he wouldn't eat unless it was scheduled into his day and now here he was moving to another state with no idea of what came next. It was so unlike him.

And it felt good.

He was sick of scheduling every moment; sick of always needing to know what the future held. He wanted to be happy and enjoy his life.

And that started with Cedarville.

It was just after three when he pulled into Carly's—now his— home. There were several other cars in the drive and, he assumed from talking to Carly earlier, that it was her cousins coming to help him unload. Stepping out of the truck he was hit with the crisp, fall, lake air. Tipping his head back, he closed his eyes and breathed it in. There was just something about this town and how it made him feel.

With his eyes closed, he heard a commotion and, when he opened them, Reed and Max, Carly's dog, came barreling toward him.

"You're here, you're here!" Reed shouted and tackled his legs while Max stopped and sniffed his feet.

"I'm here, buddy." He stroked the back of his head. When he looked back up, he saw Carly and Tony standing on the porch watching. Lifting his hand, he waved. "I made it."

"And in one piece," Carly said as she began walking toward him, Tony following. "Reed has been driving us crazy the last three hours asking when you'd be here."

"I bribed him with ice cream and it still didn't stop his asking for long," Tony added. Reed let go of his legs and Carly took his place, giving him a big hug.

"We are so happy you're here." She was smiling ear to ear, her enthusiasm for him being there completely genuine.

When she stepped back, Tony shook his hand. "It's good to have you here, man. Reed has missed you."

When he'd made the decision to move, he'd had to spend another two weeks in Baltimore before he could get back to Cedarville. So he'd left Reed with Carly again, so it would go faster and smoother.

But he'd missed him and was glad to finally be back.

"Should we start unpacking the truck?"

Carly scoffed and Tony rolled his eyes. "Seriously? You know me better than that by now. Come inside and relax first. We'll deal with that," she waved her hand at the truck, "later."

Inside the house, Ryan was greeted by the rest of Carly and Tony's friends, Brandon, Leah, Logan, and Melanie. He'd met them all several times and liked them, which was probably good, because it seemed like they hung out together as a group, a lot.

"Another city person who we have converted to small-town living," Melanie said from her spot on the couch. "Pretty soon everyone is going to want to live here."

"Please, God no," Brandon said. "More people means more crime and I am happy with the little that we have in town."

"As a public servant in this town, I would think you would want more people living here." His girlfriend, Leah said.

"Perish the thought." He exaggerated a shudder as they all laughed.

"Now that you're here," Logan said, "have you given any thought as to what you might do?"

"Dammit, Logan." Carly smacked the back of his head. "I told you to let the man breathe before you started hounding him with questions."

"How was THAT hounding him? All I did was ask a simple question." He rubbed the spot on his head Carly had hit.

"It's okay," Ryan said, chuckling. "No need to beat around the bush on my account. I know it's crazy that I moved here and I don't even have a job yet."

"It's not crazy at all," Leah said. "I moved here and while yes, I technically had a job, I had no clue what I was doing or wanted to do. All I knew was that I needed to get out of New York."

"That's how I felt," he answered honestly. "Baltimore was just not the place for me, and once I realized it, I needed to get out as fast as possible."

"I know it's not permanent," Logan said, "But if you wanted something to do the next few weeks, I could put you to work. The gallery is slated to open the week after Thanksgiving and there is still a ton of work."

"What kind of work?" Ryan had never really been a manual labor kind of guy. Yes, he could use a hammer and screwdriver, and if he needed, he could change a tire. But that was the extent of his knowledge.

"You could take over for me helping Alice," Leah said. "You'd know more about permits and building codes and tax documents than I would. Opening the dance studio was one thing, but Logan is going to have clients from all over the world, and I am just not sure of the legalities of international sales."

"I'm not licensed yet here in Ohio, so I can't do anything that would require my legal services.."

"It's not," Logan said. "I have a business lawyer when I need anything legal. This is more paperwork and codes. Mom is doing great and Leah has been a huge help, but with your expertise, we would know that everything was done correctly."

It sounded interesting and fun, and because it was only for a few weeks, it could give him time to put out feelers and plan for his future. "Let me sleep on it. I'm interested but I don't want to jump right into anything without thinking."

"No," Carly said abruptly. "No thinking. That's what your problem is, you think too much. Take the leap and just decide."

"Carly," Tony said in a warning voice, "it's his life. He can decide how to live it without your interference."

"No," he shook his head, "she's right. I wanted a change and it starts now." He turned to Logan. "I'll do it."

Logan nodded and saluted him with his beer. "I promise, it'll be painful, and as an added bonus, it'll put you in contact with people that might be able to help in your quest to start over."

Ryan liked the idea more and more. He could get his feet wet in Cedarville and start meeting people. This was a perfect way to start his new life.

Brandon stood. "Let's go get this truck unloaded. Then we can eat pizza."

Together the seven of them unloaded the truck of the things that he was keeping at Carly's house. He had a lot of furniture that wasn't needed immediately so once everything else was unloaded, he and the rest of the men drove to a storage unit to pack it away. One day, hopefully, he would get his own place and need all his furniture again. But for now, he was content to store it away.

They dropped off the truck to a local branch of the company he'd rented it from and all rode back to Carly's in Tony's truck. When they walked in the house, the ladies were all sitting on the floor around the coffee table, already eating pizza.

"Sorry," Melanie said with her mouth full, "we were hungry and couldn't wait." Logan strolled over, took the piece of pizza from her hand and took a giant bite.

"You're forgiven," he said around the bite.

Carly passed out plates as Tony grabbed beer for all the guys. Laughter and conversation flowed as it always did when they were all together. Ryan had assumed he'd feel like an outsider, but he never did. They wouldn't let him. It wasn't in their nature to leave anyone out.

"Hey, Tony," Leah said. "Where's Addison tonight?"

Hearing Addison's name stopped him cold, beer halfway to his mouth.

"No idea. I invited her as did Carly, but she never got back to me and told Carly that she had plans."

"You know what plans means, right?" Logan said. "That's a date."

Ryan about choked on his beer, but hid it by pretending to cough. Was that true? Did Addison have a date?

He'd worked so hard to push her out of his mind the last two weeks. He made sure she wasn't the reason he'd decided to move his whole life to Cedarville. But, that didn't mean he wanted to hear about her with another man. And sure, technically, they were nothing. Barely even friends. But he felt that it was more, he wanted more.

Addison Scott was Tony's sister. Ryan had met her the first time he'd come to visit Reed, after his first week in Cedarville. He'd been taken aback by her beauty first but, once they'd started talking, he found out they had a lot in common. The big one was that they both wanted more from life. Their attraction, which had been instant and mutual, only grew the more time they spent together. But Ryan hadn't been in a place where he could start something with anyone, let alone her. She was the sister of the man whose girlfriend was co-parenting Reed with him. That was as convoluted as it sounded, and made Addison completely off-limits.

And Ryan miserable.

The night that he'd come to town to take Reed back to Baltimore with him, he'd had a mini freak out and stormed out on Carly. His instinct had been to go see Addison. It was stronger than any instinct he'd ever had, but he'd forced it way down inside his mind, back to the deepest darkest pits and left it there, never to be found again.

Except that wasn't possible. One, because what he felt was too all-consuming to hide forever, and two, he'd just moved to the town next to hers, where he'd be seeing all her friends and family practically daily.

Great fucking idea.

So that night, instead of going to see her, he'd driven to the lake and sat on the shore to think. He thought about what he wanted from his life and what he wanted for Reed. He thought about how much he hated his job and dealing with all the pompous asses who worked in his firm. He thought about all the things he'd missed while climbing the corporate ladder; friends, social life, fun.

That was the night he'd decided to make a change. He hadn't known at the time that the change would be moving to Cedarville...closer to her, but that was what had come from his epiphany.

Now that he was there, he was going to have to find a way to deal with his attraction for her without doing anything about it.

So far, it was a draw on whether or not moving had been a good idea.

Chapter 2

Mornings were not her favorite time of day, especially Mondays. But Addison got up anyway the first time her alarm went off. She had a meeting at eight with a possible new client, and she wanted to make a good impression.

Padding down the short hallway of her one-bedroom apartment, she turned on the coffee pot and popped a bagel in the toaster. She had to drink coffee and eat something first thing in the morning or she'd be a total bitch to everyone for several hours. She hated it, had tried to change it, but unfortunately, it was what her body demanded of her.

With her bagel and coffee in hand, she sat down at her tiny, two-seater table. As she ate, she scrolled through her Facebook and Twitter feeds to see what was happening in the world. It had been two days since she'd been on social media, having taken a small break from online life. She did that sometimes, just to refresh and not become reliant on it for daily use. Life was too short to spend it always on your phone.

As she scrolled, her phone beeped with a message.

Carly:

I gave you 2 days, but time is up. Answer me, or I'm telling Anthony that you like Ryan

As threats went, it was a good one.

Carly, along with Leah and Mel, were the only ones she'd told of her attraction to Ryan. But she'd also told them she had no plans to do anything about it. And sure, that was before Ryan had chosen to move to Cedarville so he and Reed could live there permanently, but whatever. She wasn't thinking about that.

Or, so she lied to herself thirty times a day.

Ryan Ball was a complication she didn't need. She'd say she didn't want him, but that was another lie, and she refused to lie to herself on more than one thing.

The man was serious, like off the charts, hot. And his heart, his great, big, gigantic heart that had taken in a small boy when there was no other option—how was her own heart supposed to hold out against that?

No seriously. She needed to know.

In all her twenty-seven years, she had never met a man who seemed to care as much as Ryan. And, while it was one of the reasons for her attraction to him—hello, he was gorgeous—It was also part of the problem. He cared too much what people thought. He was always doing things because that's what he thought people wanted, instead of just doing things for himself or because he wanted to.

Addison wasn't sure she could handle that. She rarely did anything that she didn't want to do and didn't give a damn if it fit with other people's expectations. She'd done that in high school because it was the only way to make people like her. But, she'd never do it again. She was who she was, everyone else be damned.

Addison:

Do what you have to do, but there is nothing to talk about.

As much as she didn't want her brother to know that she had "sorta feelings" for Ryan, she also wasn't going to talk it to death with Carly. So what that he'd moved to Cedarville and now lived only twenty minutes from her? He had Reed to think about and she wouldn't do anything to jeopardize that relationship.

Carly:

Liar. You're such a liar that I'm guessing the fire department is on their way to your house right now because your pants just went up in flames.

Addison:

For your information, I am not wearing pants.

Carly:

I bet if you texted that to Ryan, his pants would catch fire.

Addison couldn't stop the laugh from coming out. Carly was a pain, but she was also a great person, and she was so happy Tony had found her. They were perfect together, both of them always needing to be right.

Carly:

Seriously though, I don't want you digging back into your hole and never coming out. Now that we are friends, I love having you in my life. Just because Ryan is here too doesn't mean you shouldn't come around. I know that's why you didn't come Saturday.

Addison didn't want that either. All her life she'd had a hard time making friends because of her looks. She'd been born with fantastic genes and, because of that, she was what other people called beautiful. It wasn't something she cared about, but other women did. They never wanted to be friends with her because they thought she would steal their boyfriends or husbands. Women had actually said that to her, like being beautiful gave her no self-control. It was ridiculous, and insulting not only to her, but to their boyfriends and husbands as well.

Because of that, she had remained friendless most of her life until Tony had introduced her to Carly, who in turn introduced her to Leah and Melanie. They didn't care if you were prettier, skinnier, taller, shorter, or had more or less money. They liked people because of how they acted and treated others. It was how friendship was supposed to be.

And for her, they'd been a lifesaver. She had been sick of spending every Friday and Saturday night at home, or worse, with her parents. Carly was right, and as much as that irked her, she didn't want to go back to hanging with her mom and dad.

Hot guy with a big heart was just going to have to get used to seeing her.

Addison:

As much as it pains me to say you are right...how bout I come by for lunch today?

Carly:

See you then!

Setting her phone aside, Addison finished her breakfast and got ready for work. Tony would be sitting in on the meeting since he owned the company and this was a big contract. But, since she'd secured the meeting, he was letting her take the lead.

Her work life and her social life were finally looking up. That only left her love life, and since she couldn't lie to herself again that day and say that she wasn't at all thinking about it, she instead pushed it to the back of her mind for another day.

Really though, did it count as a second lie when all the lies had to do with the same person?

When she arrived at the office, she found Tony already there, sipping coffee in his office.

"Morning, Boss." She loved calling him that because it annoyed him. And annoying him was the best part of her day.

"Stop," was all he said, not even looking up.

She glanced at the clock and noted that she still had plenty of time. Taking a seat in front of his desk she asked, "How was your weekend?"

"It was good. Reed was so excited to have Ryan back, he could barely control himself."

Hearing Ryan's name made her panic on the inside. She held strong though on the outside so Tony wouldn't ask her six billion questions. She knew that Tony suspected there was some chemistry between her and Ryan, but with him now living close, she wasn't ready – who knew if she ever would be – to deal with her feelings.

"That kid couldn't be any cuter if he tried. I'm sorry I missed his excitement." She was too, even if she had purposefully stayed away. She wasn't ready to see Ryan again, and she definitely wasn't ready to see him with a huge group of people around who would dissect every move she made.

"He missed you." Tony didn't say it with any annoyance or even questioning in his voice. Just the truth as he saw it.

"I'll make sure I go by one day this week and see him." And she would. She missed him and it had been almost a week since she'd seen him. "With Ryan living at Carly's now, do you think you will be spending more time at your place?" She was surprised by how well she'd said his name without her voice changing.

He pursed his lips. "I'm not really sure." He rubbed his fingers against his chin. "I had an idea last night but I'm not sure if anyone would go for it."

"Let me hear it."

"I was thinking that when Ryan is ready and Carly too, maybe I could just move in with Carly and Ryan could take my house here in Woodridge."

Her mouth opened but no words came out. Even just the possibility of Ryan living in her town had her tongue-tied. She could barely control her feelings for him when he'd lived five hundred miles away. If he lived a mile from her, she'd have a nervous breakdown.

Fuck her sideways.

Pulling herself together, she said, "Would you really want to give up your house?"

He shrugged. "For Carly, yes. Cedarville is more important to her than Woodridge is to me. And, because I travel so much for work anyway, it doesn't matter so much that my office is here."

Biting her bottom lip, she looked down at her feet. "What if I wanted to live in your house?"

"You want my house?" His shocked voice forced her head up and her eyes made contact with his.

"I don't know." She shook her head. "I was with you the day you found it, remember?"

"I do." He smiled. "We were going to get something for mom, weren't we? And, when we drove by you shouted at me to stop."

"I saw it and I just knew it was the perfect house. And I was right."

"You were. And it is a great house, but if it comes down to the house or Carly, I would choose Carly every day." He tilted his head and studied her. "If you want it, Addie, it's all yours. Ryan can find his own place as he planned."

"I don't know if I'm ready to own a house. It's a pretty big step."

He stood. "How about I promise not to do anything for a couple of weeks, and in that time, you can think about it?"

"Deal." She stood, glancing at her watch. "I guess I should go get ready for this meeting."

"Let me know when you are ready to start and I'll sit in."

She nodded and walked out to her desk.

When she'd first started working for Tony, she'd been his assistant. She'd been fine with that role and with her desk being in the lobby. But now that she was taking on a bigger role, and her own clients, she felt like she deserved more. There was only one problem. The office space currently only had one office and a conference room. There was also a back room where they stored equipment for installs, but that wasn't big enough either.

She didn't want to cause an issue, so for now she was keeping her mouth shut. Soon she would broach the subject with Tony and together they could come up with something.

In the meantime, she had a job to do. And she was determined to hit it out of the park.

"That went better than expected," Tony said as they watched the clients walk down the sidewalk through the glass door.

"It really did, didn't it." She turned to him. "I can't believe they signed the contract today." She was brimming with excitement and could barely contain herself. She wanted to jump up and down and hoot and holler.

He touched her shoulder. "You exceeded my expectations. I have really underestimated you and what a value you are to me and this business."

"Thanks, Tony." She smiled. "I want to be valuable and make a difference."

"You are both of those things." He stepped back. "Now, you better go if you want to make your lunch with Carly."

She rolled her eyes. Of course Carly had told him they were having lunch. She grabbed her bag, waved goodbye, and headed for Cedarville. The whole drive, she played over and over what she wanted to say to Carly. And when she stepped out of her car, she was ready.

Until she walked into Dragonfly Dance and found not only Carly, but Leah and Melanie also.

She was no match for the three of them together.

"Hey guys," she said as she entered the office. Each of them was sitting at their own desk, and they all turned when she greeted them.

"Oh thank God," Melanie said. "Leah was trying to make me do paperwork against my will. It was bad. Really bad."

"Jeez," Leah huffed out. "I ask you one little favor and you drama it all up."

"See what I have to put up with, day in and day out?" Carly asked with an eye roll.

"You love it, so don't even try to complain to me." She found a chair in the corner and took a seat. "What's the plan for lunch, cause I'm starving?"

"I called over to the deli and placed an order. Annie said she would bring it by when it's ready," Leah said. "She should be here anytime."

Addison nodded and dropped her purse on the floor since she was staying there for lunch. "So what's new?"

"Oh no. No you don't," Carly said. "Don't even try to ignore the elephant in the room."

"Is this elephant immaculately dressed, never ungroomed, and now living in Cedarville?" Melanie raised her eyebrows.

Addison made a noise that sounded like a combination of a groan and a growl. "Can we just leave the elephant in the box and never take it out?"

"Can we please stop referring to Ryan as an elephant?" Leah asked. "Every time I see him, I'm now going to picture him as an elephant wearing a three-piece suit. Then I'll laugh in his face, and he'll think I'm a crazy person."

"I'm guessing he already thinks all of you are crazy," Addison said. "But for the sake of Leah, we can stop referring to him as an elephant."

Leah gave her a thumbs up. "Nice to have someone on my side."

Carly waved her arms over her head like she was landing a plane. "Addison, if you don't start talking, and like ten minutes ago, I'm not gonna be able to take it."

"What do you want to know?"

"For starters," Melanie said, "where were you yesterday? And if you lie to us, we will know."

She wanted to roll her eyes, and maybe, take back being friends with them, but then she remembered her lonely life was without friends, and decided against both. "I was at home."

"You chose to stay home alone instead of coming to hang out with us?" Leah asked. "It's worse than we thought then, isn't it?"

"It's not bad, and it's not really a problem. I just thought it would be better if I wasn't there on his first day in town."

"But, it is a problem if you're avoiding him," Carly said. "Believe me, I know. Hell, we all know."

"Carly is the biggest avoider of all of us," Melanie said. "She could have won a gold in the Olympics."

Carly threw a towel at Mel. "Like you can talk. You literally stopped going places so you wouldn't have to talk to Logan."

"Can we all just agree that we are all avoiders and move on from there?" Leah asked. She turned to Addison. "I think the big question here is, why are you avoiding Ryan? We all know why we avoided our guys. We were in love and refused to admit it."

Sucking her bottom lip into her mouth, Addison stayed quiet.

"We know you like him," Carly said. "But is it more? Have you had any contact with him other than when we've all been together?"

She shook her head from side to side. "None." She swallowed. "That's only made it worse."

"Made what worse?" Leah asked.

"The want. I want him with a desire I have never felt before, and honestly, I'm afraid I might not ever feel again. And, that fucking scares me to death. What if he's it, and if I don't jump now, I will never have the chance again?"

"A month ago," Carly started, "I understood why you weren't willing to take a chance on something between the two of you. But, now that he lives here, I don't get it. What's holding you back?"

"Reed is. And, you and Tony. What if we start something but it's not a forever kind of something? I'll be the odd man out. And seriously guys, I can't go back to having no friends."

"Fuck me sideways," Mel cursed. "You are not going to lose us. Yes, at first if it didn't work out, we'd have to only hang out when Ryan wasn't around or without him, but then it would get better."

"How do you know that?"

"Ross and Rachel made it work," Leah said. "And, so did Ted and Robin."

She laughed. "Those are your examples? Seriously? They're characters on TV shows. Plus, Ted pined for Robin for years." She stopped talking and sat forward in her chair. "Oh, God, what if I pine for him for years?"

"What if," Carly said, "you stop being a big baby and go do something about the feelings you currently have for him? We can worry about everything else down the road."

"Carly's right, Addison. You need to take this chance to see if the feelings you have for Ryan are real, or hell, if he even has the same ones."

"Umm, we know he has the same ones," Melanie said. "He pretty much told Carly he did."

"Everyone stop," Carly demanded. "Addison," she said quietly. "There has to be something else holding you back. You are a smart woman, and you know as well as we do, that your excuse is just that...an excuse. So what gives?"

She avoided eye contact with her friends by looking down at her feet. She didn't want to tell them, but knew that if she did, they would in no way judge her or make her feel like a lesser person. So, she sucked in a breath and let the words come.

"I've never had sex more than once with a person."

Leah was the first to respond. "So you've only ever had one night stands?"

"No," she stated definitively. "I've been in relationships, but once we had sex, they broke up with me."

"So they were all asshats," Mel said.

"They weren't though." She swallowed the lump in her throat. "I'm bad at sex."

"That's ridiculous," Carly said. "Look at you, you can't possibly be bad at sex."

"In case you were unaware, being pretty does make you automatically good at sex."

"Back up a minute," Mel said. "Why do you think they broke up with you because you were bad at sex?"

"I didn't, at first. But, after the third boyfriend dumped me the day after our first time, I put two and two together?"

"No one actually said anything?" Carly asked.

"Yes and no," she said. "Guy two said that he wanted someone more experienced, and then, guy three said that we, and I quote, weren't a match."

"What the actual fuck is wrong with guys!" Leah stood and wandered the office. Addison had seen Leah in many ways, but angry wasn't one of them.

"Okay, okay, okay," Mel said. "For my own peace of mind, please tell me that you didn't let those douchebags—and they are douchebags—determine your dating life?"

"What would you have done?" She threw up her hands. "Here I was, twenty-two, and the only three men I had slept with dumped me immediately following the sex. I was the common factor in all three situations."

"Or," Leah said, "they were just idiots. No twenty year old is good at sex, male or female. It's like the law."

"True," Mel said. "I sucked at sex, and to be honest, it was never that good with anyone until Logan. I think sometimes it takes having a real connection to make it good."

"But I had a connection. With all three, we had gone out for over a month before we slept together. With the second guy, Seth, we saw each other almost daily."

"But did you love them?" Carly asked. "Or even think you might?"

She bit her bottom lip. "I liked them, but no, I don't think I loved any of them." She definitely didn't have any of the feelings she currently had for Ryan, and that's what scared her. "But I don't love Ryan, so why would it be any different?"

"You have stronger feelings for Ryan than you ever had before, right?" Carly asked.

"Yeah, I guess."

"There's no guessing to it," Mel said. "I've seen you two together and sparks fly. I feel like I'm a voyeur when you are together."

She cringed. "It is not that bad."

"Uh yeah, it is," Leah said. "It's almost worse than Carly and Tony."

"Hey!" Carly took offense. "Just because I was a blind idiot who didn't know a good thing when she saw it, doesn't mean you get to pick on me."

"Pretty sure it does mean that," Mel deadpanned.

Carly flipped Melanie off and huffed out a fake annoyed breath. Before anyone could speak again, Annie from the deli, walked through the door with their lunch delivery. As they ate, there was no more talk of Ryan or her and Ryan. Instead they told stories about their daily lives, giving advice where needed, and laughing at amusing moments.

It was what friendship was, and Addison was glad she had them, even if they were nosy bitches that were always up in her business.

Chapter 3

Pushing his hair back off his forehead, Ryan poured over the documents one more time before he had to meet with the city planner. Everything was fairly straight forward, and from what Brandon had told him, the city planner was eager to have the gallery open. So, getting ten extra parking spots added to the back of the building shouldn't be a problem.

Alice, Logan and Brandon's mom, was meeting him shortly to make sure they were ready for the meeting. She'd been great the last two days helping him get up to speed on the paperwork and the business. As an attorney, he had a lot of knowledge, but the small-town government was an entity all its own.

Standing up to stretch, he raised his arms over his head. He caught a glimpse of himself in the window and almost didn't recognize himself. He was in jeans, a t-shirt, and his feet were bare. Never in his life had he done work while wearing jeans. Hell, he'd never worked from home. But, with the gallery a madhouse, working at Carly's was easier and more productive than being on-site.

Making his way to the kitchen, he grabbed a bottle of water from the refrigerator. He'd been in Cedarville three and a half days and he was already less uptight than he'd ever been. If he'd had any reservations about moving, they were gone. Life in Cedarville was peaceful and calm. That didn't mean it was, because it wasn't. There was always something to do and with his inherited group of friends, he couldn't imagine ever being bored.

As he walked back to the kitchen table, which he was using as a makeshift desk, he heard a knock on the door. He found Alice on the other side.

"Good afternoon," he said as he shut the door behind her.

"Not sure you're going to say that in a minute." She looked frazzled.

"Is everything okay?"

"Unfortunately not. I just came from the gallery where a pipeburst. There's water everywhere and it's a gigantic mess."

"Oh wow, what can I do?"

"For starters, you are going to have to go meet the city planner alone. Logan needs all hands on deck to get this mess under control."

"Absolutely." He didn't relish going alone without knowing everything about how the town worked, but he'd go and do his best.

"And then, after that, if you could come by the gallery and help out in any way, I'm sure Logan would appreciate it. I could go pick up Reed from school and you could take my place."

He nodded. "I can do that. I assume I'll only be with the city planner for about an hour." He looked at his watch. It was already twelve-thirty and he was meeting with the planner at one-fifteen. He looked down at himself. "I guess I should go change and get ready for the meeting."

"Bring some old clothes for after. You are sure to get dirty." She opened the front door and then was gone, leaving him alone once again.

Alone and nervous.

Nervous for a meeting with a small-town city planner.

He laughed at the absurdity of it all as he walked up to his room to change. He was a rock when it came to business. It was one of the reasons he'd worked all the time. The higher-ups at his company knew they could trust him to get the job done and get it done right.

It was all so comical and ridiculous. He pulled on a pair of dress pants and found an acceptable button-down shirt. Once on, he decided to roll the sleeves hoping he'd be accepted more if he looked more casual and less big city.

So he packed up his documents, carefully placed them in his briefcase, and headed for city hall. The city planner's name was Mitch Baron and his office was on the first floor of city hall.

He found both the building and the office easily enough, but when he opened the door to Mark's office, he felt like he'd entered an alternate universe. Or, at least, some kind of eighties cartoon.

"Close the door!" someone shouted, making him quickly push the door closed.

"He's over here!" someone else yelled. "Hurry before he gets away again!"

There was a scurry of movement and three people went running toward the corner where the voice had come from.

"Got him!" someone said and held up a cage that held a small rodent-like animal.

"Oh thank God," the lone woman in the room said. "Davey would have been devastated if I'd have lost him."

"That's one fast animal," one of the men said. "You might want to fix that latch so he doesn't get away again."

"I plan on it," she said. As if finally realizing someone else was in the room she turned to him, "Oh hi. I'm so sorry you walked in on all the commotion."

"No problem."

"You must be Ryan," the tall man that had finally caught the creature said. "I'm Mark and I promise it isn't always like this around here." Ryan shook his outstretched hand. "Rebecca's nephew's chinchilla got out of his cage, and if you know anything about chinchillas, you know they are fast."

The woman in question walked closer and offered her hand to shake. "I'm Rebecca Allen, Director of Public Works. Sorry for the craziness."

"That's our Animal Control director, Darren, and our head of finance, Grant." Ryan shook both men's hands before they left and presumably retreated to their own offices.

"Come on back and we can get started." Ryan followed him into his office and took a seat in front of the desk.

"I ran into Brandon yesterday and he mentioned that he knew you. The Graham's are nice friends to have in Cedarville. They're a town staple."

"They are all really great, just like the rest of this town." Ryan wasn't sure how much Mark knew about Reed, and the relationship between them and with Carly, but he knew it wasn't a secret. "I'm so thankful for Carly and her entire family for accepting both me and my brother's son, Reed."

"From what Brandon said, you are the real hero taking the boy in."

He shrugged. "I just did what I knew was right."

After a moment of silence, Mark said, "How about we get down to business?"

They talked for almost forty-five minutes, Mark walking him through all the town procedures. He was more helpful than Ryan had assumed a public servant would be, and way more friendly. When they wrapped up, Mark even offered to stop by the gallery to see if Logan needed any more help. It seemed the news about the burst pipe had traveled through the town.

After quickly changing in the bathroom at city hall, Ryan walked the two blocks to Logan's gallery. He found a large group of people already inside, including all his friends and their families.

"Ryan, hey," Carly said when she spotted him. "Thanks for coming."

Looking around he saw what a mess the water had made. They had contained it to one side of the gallery, but still, all the flooring, walls, and equipment were soaked. "This is quite a mess."

"You're telling me." With her hands on her hips, she took in the gallery with him. "Leah, Mel, and I have to leave in a few to get to work, so any and all help is appreciated."

"Point me in the direction you need me and I'll get going."

She led him to where the guys were busy working and he jumped right in, soaking up water any way possible. For hours they worked tirelessly with people coming and going when they needed to. Mark showed up about five along with a few of Brandon's deputy's who were off duty.

At seven, Logan announced there was nothing more to do that night. "We need to wait until everything dries before we can do anymore."

"Anyone interested in pizza and beer, come on over to my house," Brandon said. "It's on me."

Almost everyone filtered out, and eventually, it was just Logan, Tony, and him.

Logan, looking worn out and defeated instead of his usual happy-go-lucky self, ran his hands through his hair. "How the fuck am I gonna have this ready in time for the opening now?"

"I know it seems impossible," Tony answered, "but we've got this. There are a lot of people in this town who are willing to help you."

"Tony's right," Ryan said. "I can give you every waking hour, and I am sure many others will do the same."

"I don't know if it's going to be enough. People were already helping me in their free time. Now I'm gonna what? Ask them for more? I don't think they have more to give."

"So push the opening back a couple of weeks," Brandon said. "It won't be the end of the world and it will take some pressure off of you."

Logan shrugged. "I need to clear my mind before I make any decisions."

"Probably a good idea," Ryan said. "And in the meantime, Brandon is buying us all pizza and beer. That's gotta help."

A small smile appeared on Logan's face. "Beer sounds like a good fucking idea."

Together they headed to Brandon's where beer was flowing and the pizza was on the way. Not everyone had come, but there were several people there that Ryan did not know or hadn't had time to meet at the gallery. Every single person was open and friendly, taking the time to introduce themselves to him.

Cedarville was in a class all of its own.

After only a beer and two slices of pizza, Ryan said his goodbyes, so he could get home and relieve Alice of Reed duty. She had been working all day too, and he didn't think it was fair to leave her with Reed all night.

He found Reed already in bed and fast asleep.

"He wanted so badly to come by and help out," Alice told him. "I used every trick in the book to keep him here."

"Maybe now that all the water is up, he can come by and help one afternoon when school is out."

"He'd love that."

She kissed him on the cheek, something his own mom used to do, and went out the front door.

After a shower and change of clothes, he fell exhausted into bed.

By noon the next day, Ryan had already put in six hours of work. He did two hours of paperwork at home before going to the gallery and getting his hands dirty. And dirty they were. They'd had to tear out the wall where the pipe burst, so the pipe could be repaired. In doing so, they had also found mold, and that made Logan want to replace the whole wall, not just the ruined part.

At that moment, he made his decision to push out the grand opening. So instead of the week after Thanksgiving, he was now going to open on New Year's Eve.

That gave him, and everyone else involved, plenty of time.

Taking a break for lunch, Ryan took his packed cooler to a card table which was set up in the back of the gallery. He mindlessly ate while reading through news from around the world on his phone. He was taking a bite of his sandwich when, from somewhere behind him, he heard the voice that haunted his dreams.

For a second, he thought maybe he was just tired, and it was a hallucination. But, when he heard it again, he turned, and sure enough, there stood Addison talking to Logan.

In an old sweatshirt that had paint stains on it, and her hair covered in a hat, she was still the most beautiful thing he'd ever seen.

If it hadn't been obvious to him before, that moment, where she was making Logan laugh, made him acutely aware of how fucked he was when it came to Addison Scott.

And if he was being truthful, how much he wanted to fuck Addison Scott.

That made him an asshole of the highest degree; that he would think something like that about her. She was better than just someone to fuck. She deserved more; more than a horny guy who masturbated to the thought of her mouth on his dick.

Okay, he had to stop, or else the whole world – or at least the people in the gallery – would know how much he wanted her.

He tried to turn back around and finish his lunch, but every time she laughed, it went straight to his dick, and he was powerless not to look at her.

And then it happened.

She turned her head and caught him staring.

He wanted to move, make it seem like he was not staring at her like a creep.

But it wasn't possible.

And then the most incredible thing happened. She smiled. At him.

Any semblance of cool went to shreds. He stumbled as he tried to stand and ended up falling on the floor. Face first.

Smooth was not his middle name.

"Holy shit!" Logan said, walking toward him. "Are you okay?" He reached out a hand as if to help him up, but Ryan shooed him off.

"Yeah, I just got my leg caught in the chair."

Logan patted him on the back. "Be careful next time. I can't afford any workers' comp claims right now." He laughed as he walked away.

"Are you sure you're all right?" Addison asked.

She was standing close, almost too close, and Ryan could smell her shampoo.

Violets.

She loved violets

"I'm fine." He wiped his hands on the front of his jeans. "Just clumsy."

"You don't strike me as the clumsy type." She tilted her head to the side and studied him. "I'd say more that you are controlled and purposeful in everything you do."

He raised an eyebrow. "You think I fell on purpose?"

"No," she smirk-laughed. "I just –" she exhaled, "you just don't seem clumsy."

"I hide it well, but I am not the most coordinated person."

"It's nice to know you aren't perfect."

He laughed, loudly. "Why in the hell would you think I was perfect?"

"You're kidding, right?" She raised both eyebrows and rolled her eyes at the same time. "Other than today, you are always dressed immaculately, your hair is never out of place and your sentences are perfectly formed."

"And spending what little time we have together, you think that gives you the right to make a snap judgment about me?" He was angry and he wasn't even sure why. He'd tried hard to cultivate his image and make it seem like he was perfect. It's what his world demanded. Show no weakness. She'd seen exactly what he'd wanted her to see.

But he wasn't in that world anymore and now, he wanted people to know the real him.

"Wow," she said, her face going from carefree to irritated. "It's nice to know how you feel." She turned and began walking away.

He grabbed her arm to stop her. "Addison, wait."

She shook her arm free of his grip. "No, Ryan. You've said what you wanted."

"But I haven't." He stepped closer to her. "Just hear me out and then you can leave. Please?"

"You have one minute." She crossed her arms over her chest.

"My whole life, I felt like I had to be perfect. My parents were...are great people, but they expected my brother and I to be exemplary and faultless. Rob was. Without trying, he got straight A's, and excelled in sports. I wasn't like that. I had to work hard just to get a B and sports were not my thing. I was uncoordinated to the point that I would trip over my own feet. One day, when I was about sixteen, I learned how to fake it. If I paid attention at all times, and never let my mind wander, I could control my awkwardness. Then I started running and lifting weights to help with sports. I still wasn't any good, but I was better and didn't trip over my own feet. After Rob dropped out of school and ran off with Tina, I felt even more of a need to be perfect. And for years, I was. Perfect job, perfect apartment, perfect clothes, and perfect hair. I was perfect...on the outside. But inside, I was still that clumsy kid. And, two weeks ago, I made the decision that being perfect was too hard. So I moved to Cedarville; a place where I could just be myself."

He was out of breath because he'd rushed to get it all out and now that he was finished, he was afraid he'd said too much.

Addison, who had listened without interrupting, looked down at her feet between them. Then she looked back up. "If it's all the same to you, I'd rather be friends with the clumsy Ryan than the perfect Ryan. Perfect Ryan only makes me more aware of all my own flaws."

He wanted to reply with something like she didn't have any flaws, but he didn't want to sound like more of an idiot. "I'm sorry I jumped down your throat. I'm still getting used to being this new person."

"Thanks for telling me. It makes me understand you better." She ran her hand down his arm in what he knew was a comforting gesture. Only to him, it felt like more. Or, maybe he just wanted it to be more.

"I should get to work." She took a step backward. "I'll see you around."

He watched her walk away, her jeans not disguising the amazingness of her ass. He wasn't sure what he expected from his first run-in with Addison, but he was positive he didn't plan on spilling his deepest secret to her.

But when she was near, he wanted to tell her everything and anything, especially if it meant she'd stay and be near him longer.

He shook his head and walked back to his lunch. It was going to be a long day with her around and him trying not to watch everything she did.

Chapter 4

Addison once again spent the day at the gallery helping in any way possible. And once again, she couldn't stop her gaze from searching out Ryan. Yesterday, after he'd told her about how he'd felt the need to always be perfect, she'd had a hard time not looking for him every second. The way he'd felt was almost the same as she had in school. She'd done everything to try and fit in when she knew deep down that it wasn't what she wanted. She loved math and wanted to spend her days doing equations and figuring out problems. Instead, she joined the cheer squad just so she'd have friends.

In high school, fitting in was everything.

But in life, it was better to be true to yourself than to be someone else, just to try and please other people.

After she'd graduated and gone to college, she'd begun to finally do the things she'd wanted. And while there were times it was lonely, she was ultimately happier.

She wanted the same thing for Ryan.

And, would it be such a bad thing if she wanted to be a part of that happiness?

Turning her head, she found him painting the newly built wall where the pipe had burst. His back was to her, so she had time to sit and watch. He was wearing a t-shirt that, if she had to guess, had never been worn for anything messy, until then. His jeans were also spotless, not an old crappy pair all guys kept for home projects or lawn mowing. As he moved the roller up and down the wall, his back muscles flexed under his shirt. Back muscles that she knew he had to have gotten from a gym and not manual labor.

It didn't matter where he'd gotten them, they were torturing her either way.

Shaking her head to bring herself back to reality, she went back to painting the trim around the door. Logan's friends and family had really pulled together, and the mess the busted pipe had caused was almost fixed. The gallery still had a lot of work to be done before it opened, making it a good thing that Logan had pushed back the date until December thirty-first.

Plus, how fun would a New Year's Eve gallery opening be?

Standing up to go get more paint, she turned with her paintbrush in hand and smacked into something.

Someone, to be more accurate.

Arms reached out to steady her, and when she looked up, she found Ryan's green eyes staring back at her.

"Now look who's clumsy." His arms were still holding on to hers and internally she was chanting, 'don't let go, don't let go.'

"I'm so sorry about that. I wasn't paying any attention." She licked her suddenly dry lips and tried to calm herself.

One of his hands dropped from where it was holding her upper arm but the other one stayed where it was. "Don't worry about it." He looked down at his shirt where she had hit him with her paintbrush. "My shirt was already a mess anyway." She saw several colors of paint stains covering the front of his shirt along with the white from her brush.

Lifting the arm that wasn't being held by his, she touched the front of his shirt. "You really made a mess of yourself, didn't you?" What should have been a short touch, and only to his t-shirt, turned into a long press of her palm to his stomach.

He looked down between them to where her hand was touching him. "Painting is not my specialty." His voice was an octave lower than it had been, and it made her stomach flip.

They stood, each of them touching a part of the other, heat coursing between them. She didn't want to move, didn't want to break the spell, but there were people everywhere.

"It's, um, it's really nice of you to help Logan out," she finally said.

"I could say the same to you. At least I don't have a full-time job to do also."

She shrugged. "Tony and I both wanted to help so we are taking turns between the office and here."

"Still, it has to be tiring." He finally dropped his hand from her arm, leaving her feeling empty.

Taking a step back to gain some control, she asked, "Have you made any life decisions yet?"

"Not yet," he said and took the paintbrush from her hand, and set it down. "Logan has asked if I could help with the paperwork, and managing of the gallery until it opens, and since I have nothing else to do, I said yes."

"Wow, that's great, Ryan. That will give you time to decide what you want to do."

"Here's hoping."

Logan walked over then. "Let's call it a day guys. I think we've done all we can do. Now we need to wait for the paint to dry."

"Works for me," she said.

"Thanks for all your help, I couldn't do this without you guys."

"No problem," Ryan said. "I'll see you tomorrow."

Logan walked away, leaving them alone once again.

"Would you want to get some dinner?" Ryan asked.

She wanted to say yes, wanted nothing more than to spend more time with him. But, she just wasn't sure she was ready. It was stupid and idiotic, but it was the way she felt. So she lied.

"I can't tonight, I promised my mom and dad I'd come by for dinner."

"Another time then," he said. "I guess I'll see you later."

"Have a good night." He walked away leaving her feeling like a fool. Why did she turn him down? He was a nice guy. A hot, sexy, nice guy who she wanted, and yet, she'd just said no to going to dinner with him.

What the hell was wrong with her?

Not wanting to answer that, she cleaned up her mess and left the gallery. Her friends were still working, so her only option was to go home. Alone.

Not what she'd have chosen, but since she turned down Ryan, there was nothing else to do.

Being alone would have to do.

By two the next afternoon, Addison had made up her mind. If she was going to have these feelings for Ryan, she was going to do something about them.

What, she had no idea.

Her first thought had been to go by his house, tell him how she felt and let the chips fall where they may. But after remembering that he lived with Carly, Tony, and Reed, she crossed that off the list.

After that, she was out of ideas.

Tony, who had been out on an install, walked into the office. He looked worn out and tired.

"Wow, you look like shit."

"It's been a long night and day." He sat down on the couch across from her desk. "Reed got some kind of stomach bug last night and woke up at eleven, vomiting all over his room. So, while Carly tended to him, Ryan and I cleaned the room and washed all the bedding. Then, he was throwing up every hour on the hour, so none of us got any sleep."

"Oh poor kid. He must be miserable."

"He was, but he pulled through like a champ. Ryan said he stopped vomiting about nine this morning and hasn't since. Carly wanted to take the day off to be with him, but with Ryan there it worked out great. I'm not sure what we'll do when he gets a job and has to go to work."

"There are enough people around who would be willing to help out, including mom."

"True."

"Why don't you go home and get some sleep? I know you were supposed to come in so I could go to Logan's, but I think Logan will understand."

He stood. "I think I might just do that." He walked to the door. "If you need me though, call."

She saluted him. "Will do!"

Alone again, she started on the bid for a supermarket that came in last week. She'd been saving it for Tony, but she had no problem doing it herself. It was a big job...a big job that she had gotten. She was feeling better and better about the fact that Tony had given her more responsibility and was letting her do almost any job that they took. She had the knowledge, and she loved the business. At first, her mom had thought she was crazy for wanting to work in security with Tony, but when she realized that Addison was good at it, and it gave her self-confidence, she jumped on board.

When she finished the proposal, she straightened up her desk, cleaned up the office, and left the building. It was after six, and because she was starving and didn't want to cook, she ran into the burger place next door and placed a to-go order. When her number was called, she grabbed her bag and headed out the door toward her car. She clicked unlock and had just gripped the handle when she heard someone say her name.

"Addison."

Startled, but only because she hadn't been paying attention, she turned and found Ryan standing on the edge of the curb.

"Holy shit, Ryan," she put her free hand against her rapidly beating heart, "you scared me."

He didn't move from where he was standing. "Sorry, I didn't mean to."

She took him in. His clothes were not neatly pressed as they usually were and his chin was starting to be covered in a layer of hair. Ryan, not shaved, was somehow ten times sexier than Ryan shaved.

And, that was trouble.

"What are you doing here?" She opened the door to her car and set her food and purse inside. Closing the door, she leaned against her car.

"Would it be weird if I said I wasn't sure?"

She glanced sideways at him, an eyebrow raised. "How can you not be sure?"

"I had a shit day. Reed was sick all last night, and today, I stayed home and took care of him. When Tony got to the house thirty minutes ago and told me to get out of the house and get some fresh air, seeing you was the only thing I wanted to do."

"You wanted to see me?"

"I always want to see you." Finally he took a step closer to her. "Is that...okay?"

Pushing off the car, she faced him head-on. "It's okay." Taking his hand in hers, neither moved. "Are you hungry?"

His eyes turned feral. "Very."

She laughed. "For food, only food." She began to walk back towards the burger place, him at her side, since they were holding hands. "At least for now."

They ordered him some food and then he followed her back to her apartment. She lived on the second floor, which was also the top floor, and together they walked the flight of stairs.

"Welcome to my ridiculously small, but very inexpensive apartment." She opened the door and let him go in before her. Shutting the door, she followed him inside.

"It's cozy."

"Cozy is just another word for small."

He turned to her. "It's just you, so it's not like you need a huge place."

"I know, but sometimes I feel like this apartment makes me a bad grown-up. Like I should have more by now."

"More how? And, what's it matter if you're happy?"

She shrugged. "I guess it doesn't." She walked to her kitchen, which was only a few steps away. "What do you want to drink? I have water, beer, and soda."

"I think I'll stick to water."

She grabbed two and met him at the couch where he was already unpacking their food. "How was Reed today?"

"Ornery. Once he stopped vomiting, he didn't understand why he needed to rest. All he wanted to do was play, and I was the bad guy because I wouldn't let him."

"Ahh, poor kid. I remember being the same way when I was sick."

"So do I, but now, as the grown up, I see how obnoxious I was."

As they ate, they talked mostly about Reed and how it was to be in Cedarville versus Baltimore. When she finished her burger she asked, "Have you thought about what you want to do for a job?"

He popped a fry into his mouth and chewed before saying, "Yes and no. As a lawyer, there are lots of ways I can go, but I think I want to help businesses get up and running. The work I am doing for Logan is interesting and I, shockingly, enjoy working alongside local government."

"That's great. I'm sure Cedarville will welcome you with open arms."

"I hope so, but I'm actually thinking about having my practice here in Woodridge."

"Here?" she almost choked on the fry she was eating.

"It's a bigger town, and while not a city, I feel like I would have more opportunities here."

She swallowed the food in her mouth. "That's...smart."

"Is that a problem? Me living here?"

"No." Her eyes went wide. "I guess I just never thought you'd choose Woodridge over Cedarville."

"I'm not choosing one over the other. I'll have work in both. But Woodridge has a lot of appeal to it." He paused. "You live here, you should know."

"I grew up here, so aside from college in Columbus, this is all I've known."

"But do you like living here?" It should have been an easy question for her to answer. But somehow, she wasn't sure.

"It's nice, and I like being near my family."

"Wow, what a stunning review. You should write the brochures, tourism would skyrocket."

"Are you making fun of me?" She knew he was and liked that his sense of humor was finally showing.

"I absolutely am." A smile lit up his face. "Seriously though, do you not like living here?"

"I do, really. It's just that I didn't get a choice. It was made for me before I was even born."

"After college you could have moved somewhere else though, but you came back here."

"Because I was afraid. Woodridge is comfortable to me. So I took the easy way out and came back."

"If you weren't afraid, if there was nothing stopping you, where would you live?"

"That's just it, I don't even know. I'm not even sure if I would pick another place other than here. I think I just...wanted the choice."

He was silent as he played with the label on his water bottle. "It would suck if you moved now that I live close."

She wanted to lean in and kiss him. As a matter of fact, having his lips on hers was a reoccurring dream. Her only problem was her mind kept going to her insecurities of being bad at sex.

When his hands came up and cupped her face, the decision was an easy one. "You're thinking too hard," he said, his breath mixing with hers."

"Make me stop," she murmured and closed the distance. When his lips touched hers, she melted. All the thoughts of being bad disappeared. His lips were tender yet strong, and in her limited experience, they were the gold standard of lips.

His hands continued to hold her face, but she needed to touch him. Lifting her arms, she gripped his biceps and held on. The kiss went on, both of them willing participants.

When he finally slowed and pulled back, they were both out of breath. He looked like he was about to apologize, so she stopped him.

"If you tell me you are sorry that happened, I will kick your ass."

He smiled, a huge, whole face smile. "I'm not in the least bit sorry. I've been thinking about kissing you since the moment you walked into Carly's house the night we met."

She bit her bottom lip. "You have some serious self-control."

"I really don't." He dropped his hands from her face forcing her own to fall into her lap. "I'm not great at saying the right thing, unless it has to do with business, but I need to tell you something."

"I'm listening."

"I've never been in what most people consider a relationship. I've dated, and yes, I've had sex, but nothing ever lasted more than a couple weeks. But I want to try. With you. That is, if you wanted?"

He seemed so nervous, and looked like this was the hardest thing he'd ever done. So, she put him out of his misery.

"I've only been in two very short relationships. Like only a month long." She waited for his reaction.

A slow smile grew on his face. "So basically, we are two losers who have no clue how to be in a relationship?"

"So it seems."

"Maybe that's a good thing. Maybe we can learn together?"

Her hands fidgeted in her lap. "What if we mess it up?"

"What if we don't?"

She eyed him curiously. "I wouldn't have taken you as an optimist."

He laughed. "I never have been. But, I figure enough crazy shit has happened to me in the last year – hell, six months – to last a lifetime. I'm due for something amazing."

"And I'm that something?"

He ran his thumb across her bottom lip. "I'm hoping so."

Her chest was rising and falling at a fast pace, the excitement of actually going for it with Ryan was almost too much to take. But there was still one problem...sex. She wouldn't be able to take it, if she lost what she could have with Ryan, all because she sucked in the bedroom.

"I have one rule," she blurted out.

His eyebrows raised and his hand, which was still touching her bottom lip, dropped. "I didn't know we got to make rules?"

"There should always be rules."

"And here I thought I was the uptight one."

"Making fun of me is not a great way of getting on my good side."

"I've seen your good side, and without being crude, it looks great in a pair of jeans."

She tried not to laugh, but it was futile. Plus, it pleased her that he found her ass to his liking. To her it was and always had been too big. Not Kardashian big, but normal big.

"Be serious for one second." She touched his thigh with her hand. "I want to go slow." At his quizzical look she added, "As in no sex."

She watched his face for annoyance or displeasure. But it didn't come. "As much as I want to argue with you and disagree, the practical part of me knows it's a good idea. Rushing into anything isn't going to make either one of us suddenly good at relationships."

Relieved that he was okay waiting, she let out the breath she had been holding. "So we're agreed. We'll do this but we'll take it slow."

He nodded. "I do believe we have a deal." He looked down at his lap. "I guess I should probably get going." He started to stand, but she grabbed his hand to stop him.

"Unless you have to for some reason, why don't you stay for a while. We could talk, or watch TV or something else if you want." She hated that she sounded desperate and needy, but she didn't want her time with him to end. Not yet.

"I'd love to stay and do, well anything, I just didn't want to overstay my welcome."

"You're not. Let's just take time to get to know each other."

She reached for his hand, gripping it tight in her own. She hoped that by getting to know each other better, when they finally did have sex, he'd like her enough to forgive how bad she may or may not be.

Chapter 5

For the first time in who knows how long, Ryan was going out on a date. And all the more awesome...it was with Addison. When he'd left her house on Thursday night after hours of talking, he'd asked if she would like to go out with him.

The giant smile that had covered her face, had been enough of an answer for him, or so he'd thought. But, when she shyly answered yes, he'd felt like a teenager all over again.

As did he the moment he'd tried to pick out something to wear. He'd already changed his shirt three times and his pants once. He was rethinking the khakis he'd just changed into when someone knocked on his door.

"Come in." He dropped the jeans he was holding back onto the bed.

"Hey," Carly said, stepping into his room. "Holy shit, what happened in here?"

He looked around at the mess he'd made as he'd tried to pick out something to wear.

"How the hell do people decide what to wear on a date?" He felt like a loser and a freak for being so nervous.

Carly walked further into his room, picked up one of his discarded shirts from his bed and sat down. "I think you need to relax."

"If it was as simple as that, don't you think I'd have done it by now." He shook his head and sat down next to her. "How did I make it to thirty and not know how to date?"

"You've been busy. Plus, I think it has more to do with who you are going on a date with rather than not knowing how to date. Addison is important, and in here," she touched the side of his head, "you know that."

He gave her a tentative smile. "She is important and I don't want to do anything to mess this up."

"The only way you can mess up is by not relaxing and not being yourself. Addison has seen you dressed many times. She knows what she is getting into. I promise you, your outfit will have no bearing on whether or not this date goes well."

"What you're saying is if the date goes badly it's because my personality sucks?"

She gave a sarcastic shake of her head and said, "Yes, that's absolutely what I am saying." She slapped his arm. "She already likes you, Ryan. Stop worrying, put on one of these shirts and go have a good time."

"It's really that easy?"

"It really is."

Standing, he grabbed the shirt he'd put on originally and changed into it.

"Sisterly advice out of the way, I actually came up here to warn you about Tony."

"What about Tony," he asked as he buttoned his shirt.

"He wants to talk to you about dating his sister."

His eyes widened and he stood frozen in place. "Is he...angry?" Ryan had never seen Tony angry. Just the opposite actually. He seemed so easy going most of the time.

"I hate to say it, but I'm not sure. He wouldn't tell me. I know he is protective of Addison but honestly, I didn't think he'd have a problem with you two dating."

He frowned, wondering if he'd misjudged Tony. "I guess I should go face the music." Leaving his room, he and Carly made their way downstairs.

"Reed," she said as soon as they stepped into the living room, "why don't you and I go outside?"

Reed leaped at the chance and skipped after Carly, Max hot on his heels.

"Hard to believe that's the same boy who only twenty-four hours ago was vomiting every two minutes."

Tony stood up from where he'd been on the floor playing with Reed. "It's amazing how fast kids bounce back."

He seemed relaxed, but that didn't stop Ryan from being nervous. He couldn't recall ever having a conversation with a date's family member. Even in high school, no one had ever warned him off. He was the good kid, the kid that every parent wants their child to date. Only he hadn't really wanted to date. He'd been too busy trying to be perfect.

"Addison mentioned that you and she were going out tonight." His hands were in his pockets and he still seemed relaxed.

Ryan on the other hand was afraid he'd have to go change his shirt because he was about to sweat through it. "We are. Is that," he swallowed, "okay?"

"Relax, Ryan, I am not trying to interfere or give you the 'if you hurt my sister' speech. I only wanted to tell you that she isn't a big dater. I actually don't remember the last time she went on a date or at least told me about it. So while I'm worried about her, I am also worried about you. We're friends, hell close to family, and you've just gone through a huge change in your life. I don't want you to jump into anything you aren't ready for."

Ryan exhaled. "I appreciate that you are worried about me. I think of you and Carly like family too. But I'm good. More than good, surprisingly. I know I've only been here a week, but it's like a weight has lifted off my shoulders. I think this town has some sort of magical powers."

"You joke, but I wouldn't be shocked to find out it's true."

They both laughed before Tony said, "Go have fun and forget I ever went all 'dad' on you."

"It looks good on you, maybe you and Carly should try it out." He slapped Tony on the back as he walked by him. "Tell Reed I'll see him tomorrow."

He left the house feeling lighter than he had all day. A date that he'd been dreading – not because of the person but because of his own self-doubt – he was suddenly eager to go on. He'd told Addison he'd pick her up at seven, leaving him just enough time to stop at the store and buy her flowers.

Violets. They were her favorite, or at least that's what she had told him one of the first times they had met. He didn't remember how it'd come up or why, but he'd certainly remembered her answer. And her smell. She always smelled of violets.

He'd called ahead to a local flower shop in Woodridge to make sure they'd had some available, but they shocked him when he walked in and they'd pre-made what could only be described as a gorgeous bouquet. Over two dozen violets along with many other accent flowers and that green stuff all flowers had.

Baby's something or other.

The florist waited anxiously for him to decide if he wanted the bouquet that she'd worked so hard on. Without making her wonder, he slid his credit card across the counter.

"It's perfect. Thank you."

Taking the flowers, he got back in his car and drove the last three miles to Addison's place. He took the steps two at a time, quickly knocking on her door. All of a sudden, he didn't want to wait for another second to see her.

Seeing her was the best part of his day.

The door swung open before he barely finished knocking. Making him think she was, hopefully, as excited to see him, as he was her.

"Hey," they both said at the same time, him breathing a little heavier due to his run up the stairs.

She looked...words escaped him. Beautiful was too tame a word with how amazing she looked. She was wearing a pair of tight black jeans or maybe they were just pants. He wouldn't know without touching the material. Maybe that would happen later. Her top was a deep purple sweater, that swooped low at the neck and was accented by a low, cleavage hanging necklace.

He was having a hard time not staring at where the necklace was hanging.

It was a place he desperately wanted to be.

"You're gorgeous," he said when he finally got his brain and his mouth to connect.

"You look great too." She ran a hand down the front of his shirt which was visible under his open jacket. "We coordinated without even talking."

The shirt he had chosen was burgundy in color, easily matching her purple sweater. "These are for you," he said and held out the flowers.

"Oh my. Violets," she said wonder in her voice. "How did you know that violets were my favorite?"

"You told me."

She looked at him quizzically. "When?" As she spoke, she stepped back to let him inside.

He closed the door behind them saying, "One of the first times we met."

"Why don't I remember that?" She was in the kitchen, digging for what he could only assume was a vase.

"Don't laugh but I don't remember either. All I remember is that you said violets were your favorite."

She filled the vase she finally found with water. "So we had a conversation that neither of us remembers, but obviously happened because, well, violets."

He laughed. "No wonder we're both bad at dating. We can't even remember conversations we've had together."

She joined in with his laughter. "Well, I for one am glad that we had this alleged conversation. These flowers are beautiful and if I had never told you about my love of violets, you wouldn't have brought them."

"Should we head out? I made reservations at the seafood place you mentioned you liked."

"Look at you bringing flowers and making reservations at my favorite place." She picked up her jacket from the arm of the couch. "Those aren't things bad daters do."

"I'm turning over a new leaf." He opened the front door, letting her walk through first.

"I'm the guinea pig then?" She locked the door before turning to look up at him. In her heeled boots she was close to his six foot one inches in height. Only an inch or two lower.

"You're the reason, not the experiment." He reached out and took her hand in his.

She shook her head slightly left to right and pulled her upper lip into her mouth with her teeth. "You are...dangerous to my ego."

He smiled and tugged her forward. "Let's go eat and I'll let you try to return the favor."

She laughed all the way down the stairs.

They were halfway through their meal and having an engaging and pleasurable time. There were no awkward silences and no weird 'oh you like that' moments.

She was funny, smart, intriguing, beautiful, and he was having a hell of a time not falling head over heels in love with her. He kept telling himself to slow down, enjoy the moment. But then she would say or do something and his heart would start racing and his palms would sweat. Not to mention that the whole night he'd had to work hard not to stare at her cleavage, and if he did glance down, his dick would go instantly hard.

And, while he was glad to know that his dick still worked after years of no sex, he did not want a hard-on in the middle of a restaurant.

"Last night you mentioned that you don't really talk to your parents, right? Do you miss them?"

He'd told her how his parents hadn't wanted anything to do with Rob after he'd married Carly's mom, Tina. Even when they'd found out about Reed, they refused to help out or even meet him.

To them, Rob was dead even before he was actually dead. And, because Reed had come from him, they pretended he didn't even exist.

"I thought I would," he answered honestly. "But once I got to know Reed and then come to love him, it just made me mad that they wouldn't even try." He took a drink of his wine. "Kids have no control over who their parents are or what their parents do. And the fact that my own parents would turn their backs on him; no, I don't miss them."

Reaching across the table, she took his hand in hers. "You are so remarkable. I don't think I've ever met someone who is so selfless, so willing to do the right thing, even at the cost of losing his own parents."

"Being a good person isn't as hard as people make it out to be."

"Maybe someday you can teach me how."

He twisted her hand in his and bent to kiss her knuckles. "Deal." He looked up at her and caught the red flush of her cheeks. He wasn't sure if it was caused by embarrassment or heat, but he knew he liked it. "I have a question," he asked but didn't wait for her to answer. "When I first came to town, Carly mentioned that she had just met you and that you were new friends. What about your other friends?"

The hand that he had been holding, pulled out of his abruptly as she fidgeted in her seat. It was obvious that she was uncomfortable with this topic and he was pissed at himself for bringing it up.

"Nevermind. It's not important." He said it nonchalantly, hoping to ease her skittish demeanor. "How about dessert?"

"Ryan," she said his name boldly, reaching her hand back out to him. "Forgive me for being weirded out by that question. It's a touchy subject for me and I'm still learning to deal with it."

"I didn't mean to put you on the spot or to make you uncomfortable."

"I know you didn't. I'd really like to tell you if you still want to know."

"I want to know everything about you," he said seriously.

She breathed in deeply. "This is gonna sound conceited and narcissistic but, it's the only way to tell the story."

"Since you are neither of those things, I think I will be able to follow."

"A lot of women don't like having pretty friends. Or, I should say prettier than they are. They think we'll do things like take attention away from them or steal their boyfriend or husband."

His mouth dropped open but no words came out. He wanted to think that he'd heard her wrong, that she hadn't just said that women were so jealous of her beauty that they didn't want to be friends with her.

"Tell me you're joking?" he finally said.

She shook her head from side-to-side. "I wish I were."

He swallowed the lump that had formed in his throat. This smart, funny, and yes, beautiful woman, had to go without friends all because of other women's insecurities.

Life was the worst.

"They don't deserve your friendship. That's beyond reprehensible that people would do that."

She shrugged. "It used to hurt, but now that I have friends—ones who don't judge me solely on my looks—I've let it go." She gave him a half-smile. "At least I've tried to."

"Well, I'm here if you ever want someone to beat those women up." He was trying to lighten the mood, and the giant smile that appeared on her face told him it had worked.

"If you don't think Carly, Leah, and Mel have already tried to get names from me, then you don't know how they work yet."

They spent another hour enjoying more conversation and sharing a dessert. When they left the restaurant, he wasn't ready for the night to end.

"I can take you home if you want," he said as they walked to his car.

"Yeah, if you want," she answered.

He stopped walking, her taking another few steps. With her back to him, he said, "What if I don't want to though?"

She stopped and turned to look back at him. "I'm not ready to go home yet either."

He exhaled and closed the distance between them. "Thank God we are always on the same page."

She threw her head back and laughed, a deep sensual laugh. "Come on," she took his arm in hers, "let's go find something to do."

Since he wasn't familiar with the town and what it had to offer, he let her choose. And boy did she.

They ended up at the local indoor go-kart track, where for the next two hours, she proceeded to kick his ass on the track.

It was the sexiest thing he'd ever seen.

The energy and excitement she showed from racing was contagious. She lit up the room, engaging with everyone they came in contact with. He fell deeper into like with her, each second they were there.

By the time they left, they were both sweating and energized from the experience.

She spun in the parking lot, arms wide out to her sides. "That was so much fun!"

He watched in awe as she continued to spin, her face turned to the sky. How he was going to follow her one rule and 'take it slow,' he didn't know. But, because he wanted her happy all the time, he was going to do his damnedest.

Grabbing one arm, he pulled her toward him, and she ended up in his arms. "You're amazing."

She touched his face with one hand. "No, we're amazing. Somehow, I think we are better together, than we are apart."

He didn't disagree, he couldn't, because it felt so right to him. They were better together, or at least he was better because of her. Leaning in, he kissed her lips, lightly. When she deepened it, he didn't argue. No way was he missing his chance to kiss this woman.

He parted her lips with his tongue, telling himself to go slow and not overwhelm her. When her tongue met his in a fierce battle of control, he moaned into her mouth. Gripping her hips in his hands, he pulled her flush against his body, forcing her arms around his neck. They focused solely on each other, forgetting the world around them.

It felt right to have her in his arms, their lips fused together. More right than anything he could remember in his life. He never wanted it to end, but when he heard voices in the distance, he knew it was time to go back to reality.

"We have to stop," he said when he pulled back, his lips tingling from their kisses.

"Always so practical." She smiled evilly.

He gave a low chuckle. "Did you want to be caught kissing by a bunch of teenagers?"

"Not teenagers per se, but the thought of being caught does have a certain appeal."

He raised one eyebrow. "Your bad girl side is showing."

"I've never been a bad girl. Ever. Maybe that's what makes me want to try."

"And being caught making out is something bad girls do?"

"It's a start." She shrugged. "We can work our way up from there."

He laughed as they started walking toward his car. "Not being bad is something else we have in common. I've never took the chance to be anything but good." He opened the passenger side door for her.

Sitting down, she tucked her legs into the car and looked up at him. "Something else we get to learn together."

Ryan drove her home and walked her up the one flight of stairs, until they were standing at her door.

"I had a really great time," she said.

"Me too."

"I assume you are going to Leah and Brandon's tomorrow afternoon?"

Brandon had mentioned that he and Leah were having everyone over for the last grill out of the season—even though it was already November—and, if the weather held, maybe a bonfire.

"I will be there. I could pick you up if you'd like?"

"That'd be silly, you are already in town."

He smiled. "Let me rephrase that. I would love to come pick you up."

She leaned in and kissed his lips lightly. "I'd love that." He deepened the kiss, and this time with no one around or possibly watching, he gave her everything he had. It went on and on, he wished it would never end. But, when it did, it pleased him to see her hesitate before entering her apartment. He knew she liked him and that she wanted him. He didn't plan on pushing her on the taking it slow thing, but it did wonders for his ego to know that he probably could, if he wanted to.

The smile on his face stayed the whole ride home to Cedarville, and when he fell into bed, his head was filled with thoughts of Addison.

Chapter 6

Addison danced around her apartment as she cleaned. The music was blaring or at least it was as loud as she could have it without the neighbors complaining. She hated cleaning, only doing it when she had to, but Ryan had put her in such a great mood the previous night that she didn't even care that it was her scheduled cleaning day.

Their date had gone amazingly well. Who knew that was what dating was supposed to be like? Not her, that's for sure. She had never had someone be so attentive toward her, actually caring about what she was saying. And, she knew it wasn't just an act for Ryan. That wasn't how he was made.

And the kisses? Holy moly, had they turned her on. She hadn't been joking when she'd told him that being caught would be exciting. It was true. When they'd started the kiss in the parking lot, she hadn't given any thought to where they were, but after a few minutes, it hit her and made the kiss that much more exciting.

Although, it had been a miracle that she'd been able to think at all. The man could kiss. What was even more amazing, was that he didn't seem to think she was the worst kisser on the planet, and he was turned on by them. She could tell from the rather large erection that had been pressed against her stomach.

An erection that had her debating whether or not her no sex rule was a dumb idea.

Finishing up her tiny living room, she moved on to her bedroom. Stripping her bed of the sheets, she dropped them into her washer. Having a washer and dryer in her apartment had been a must when she'd looked for a place to live after college. Walking up and down stairs just to wash a pair of pants hadn't appealed to her.

She spent the next two hours, folding and putting away clothes, most of which were on her floor because she hadn't been able to pick out an outfit for her date with Ryan. Even for the casual cookout that night, she was unsure of what to wear.

She knew, in the recesses of her brain, that if a guy didn't like you because of your clothes, then it wasn't worth it. But, she was a girl. A girl who liked a boy and she wanted that boy to like her, no matter what.

As she put her clothes away, she was also wondering if they would work for that night.

She heard her phone ding, indicating she had a new message. Picking it up, she saw it was from Ryan.

Ryan:

Is three o'clock okay to pick you up? Carly says the gathering starts early because they want to have some daylight left.

Addison:

Three is perfect.

Ryan:

Great. I had fun last night.

Addison:

Me too. Do you know my favorite part?

Ryan:

I know what my favorite part was...kissing you.

Addison:

The kissing was pretty spectacular but what was really hot, was me kicking your ass at go-karts and you not at all mad that you lost to a girl.

Ryan:

THAT made you hot?

Addison:

MmmHmm

Ryan:

Then you'll be all over me if we ever play any sport or hell, even a board game. I always lose.

Addison:

Stop trying to turn me on.

Ryan:

No promises. See you at three!

She sat her phone down after she re-read their conversation. He was so damn cute. And, it had turned her on when he'd lost to her, every time, and he never once complained or seemed annoyed. In fact, he'd been happy for her and told her how fantastic she was.

That had made it very hard to stick to her guns and not let him talk her into bed.

Quickly glancing at the clock, she noticed that it was after one. If she was going to be ready in time for Ryan to pick her up, she'd better start getting ready.

After a shower, blow-drying and curling her hair, putting on her make-up and once again, rummaging her wardrobe for something to wear, she was down to only five minutes before Ryan was due to show up.

She was pulling on her Uggs when she heard his knock on the door.

Standing, she fixed her sweater from where it had gone crooked before opening the door.

If possible, he was more gorgeous than the night before. Long-sleeved t-shirt, jeans, hiking boots, and a little bit of stubble on his face.

It was the stubble that had her breathing heavily.

"Hi," she smiled at him. "Let me just grab my jacket."

He stayed waiting at the door while she turned off the light and picked up her jacket. After she locked her door, they walked together down the stairs. At the bottom, she kept going and hadn't noticed that he didn't follow, until she was several steps ahead. Turning she found him staring after her.

"Is something wrong?"

Taking three large steps, he landed directly in front of her. Gripping her around her waist he swooped her into his body. "Yeah, this." When his mouth touched hers it was as electric as the night before. This kiss was fast and hot, just enough to make her want more.

"I couldn't wait any longer to do that." He brushed a piece of hair from her face.

"Do you see me complaining?"

Guiding her to his car, she slid in before he shut the door. After he'd gotten in the other side and began driving he asked, "How do you want to do this today? You and me?"

"Oh, I hadn't even thought of that." She'd been too caught up in the excitement of it all to give any thought to what her friends would say. "I assume they all know that we went out, right?"

"I know Carly and Tony do, but I haven't seen anyone else to know for sure."

Turning a little in her seat so she could see him, she said, "What would you like to say?"

He gave her a quick glance. "If you're leaving it up to me, I'd tell them all that we are dating."

She touched his shoulder. "Once again, we are on the same page."

When they pulled into Leah and Brandon's, he asked her to wait so he could come around and open the door. He'd done the same thing the night before, and while old fashioned, it also warmed her heart that there were people like him still in the world.

"Let me just grab the beer I brought from the back."

"I asked Leah if I should bring anything, and she told me no. Now I feel bad."

"Don't. I only brought this because I found it in the store, and it's a local Maryland microbrew that I like. I thought others might enjoy it too."

They walked around to the back of the house because they heard noise, and sure enough, Leah, Brandon, Melanie, and Logan were all back there.

Brandon already had a fire going in his massive fire pit and he and Logan were arguing over something to do with it. Mel and Leah on the other hand were drinking wine and laughing at something.

Probably the guys.

"Thank, God," Logan said when they walked up. "Ryan, can you please come help me deal with my insane brother?"

Giving her a sideways glance, he handed her the beer. "Put this on the porch for me, will ya, while I go settle whatever those two are fighting about?"

Laughing, she took the beer and walked up to the porch.

"Did you and Ryan come together?" Leah asked, sitting forward on her lounge chair.

Opening the cooler that was on the porch, she set the beer down inside, then poured herself a glass of wine that the ladies were already drinking. "We did."

"Hold up," Mel said. "He drove to Woodridge to get you only to drive back to Cedarville?"

"You make it sound like we live hours apart."

"That's a big deal in this town," Leah said. "People here feel like driving more than ten minutes is like driving an hour."

She shook her head. "Well, Ryan isn't from this town or my town. So it's no big deal."

"Tell us about the date." Leah patted the chair next to her.

"It was great."

"By the huge smile that just popped up on your face and your glassy eyes, I'd say it was more than great."

She leaned back in her chair and crossed her ankles. "He was so sweet, starting with bringing me violets, which are my favorite flowers."

"Ahh," both girls cooed.

"Every time we got in and out of the car, he opened the door for me. He made a reservation at my favorite restaurant, held my hand when we walked. It was like a fairy tale. Oh, and are you ready for the best part? We went go-karting – my choice – and he had a great time, even after I beat him every time. He never once got pissy because he didn't win."

"Wanna switch," Melanie said. "Logan hates to lose and I am better than him at so many things."

"Bran lets me win because he loves me," Leah bragged.

They all laughed and Mel got up to refill her wine. "What else did you guys do?"

She knew what Melanie was asking; had they had sex, but before she could answer, Carly and Tony walked around the corner.

"The fun can start now!" She held two bottles of wine above her head.

Tony waved to them, but just like Ryan had, he went straight to where the guys were. Carly joined them on the porch, quickly pouring herself a glass of wine.

"What are we talking about?" she asked as she sat down next to Leah.

"Addison's date with Ryan," Mel answered.

"Oh my God, I so wanted to call you today and see how it went. But, then I saw Ryan and how happy he was, and I just knew it went well."

"It did. If I didn't already know some of his past and things that have happened to him, I'd say he was too perfect. But knowing the things I do, and seeing how amazing he still is...well, it only makes me like him more."

"More than the already halfway in love with him that you were?" Carly asked.

She nodded. "I know it's crazy and I am working overtime to keep my emotions in check."

"Don't fight it," Mel said.

"Oh really, queen of denial. You are the last one to tell anyone not to fight love." Leah swatted Mel's arm.

"And you're better?"

"I didn't say that. I fought hard against my feelings for Brandon, but in the end it all worked out."

"Same with me and Anthony," Carly said. "You all know how hard I fought that shit."

"What if I don't want to fight it," she said quietly. "When I met Ryan I wasn't looking for something permanent. But, the more I get to know him, the more I know, deep down, that he is what I want. Is that insane?" She looked at her friends, all of them listening intently.

"That's not insane at all, Addison," Carly said. "I wish that when I'd met Anthony I'd let myself fall in love immediately. I hate that we lost those six months."

"I'm a firm believer that when it's right, it's right," Leah added. "Nothing, including time, will change that."

Addison looked out to where the guys were standing around the fire. Ryan chose the same moment to look over toward her. It was almost as if he knew she was looking at him. He gave her a small head nod and a huge smile.

"Ladies, I do believe another one has bitten the dust," she heard Carly say.

When she looked back at them, they were all grinning ear to ear.

"You are in deep," Mel said.

"What are you talking about?"

"She's talking about the fact that, when you just looked over to Ryan, you showed us all your cards." Leah stood and poured herself more wine. "The look on your face was pure love."

She didn't know what to make of that and also wondered if Ryan was able to tell. More so, did she care if he could? They changed the subject, and just in time, as the guys walked up on the porch.

"What were you guys doing down there?" Leah asked.

"Men stuff, honey. You wouldn't understand." Brandon kissed her on the forehead at the same time that she swatted his arm.

"Man stuff my ass."

"Who wants a beer?" Logan asked.

"I brought a microbrew from Baltimore, if anyone wants to try it," Ryan said.

As Logan passed around the beers, Ryan came and sat down next to her. She tried to play it cool, but couldn't stop herself from looking at him and smiling like a goof.

He probably thought she was a lunatic.

"Hey," Melanie said, "where's Reed tonight?"

"He's having a sleepover at Carly's dad's," Ryan said. "He was so excited that we had to take him over early just to shut him up."

"He's not lying," Tony said. "He woke up and thought it was time to go."

They chatted a few more minutes until Brandon asked if anyone wanted to play horseshoes. Addison loved horseshoes and immediately said yes, hoping that Ryan would want to be her partner.

"I'll play too," he said looking over at her, "but be forewarned, I suck." He gave her a side wink, letting her know he remembered their earlier text conversation.

The horseshoe pits were along the side of the house but Addison chose the side closest to the fire. She wasn't cold, but the warmth from the flames felt nice.

"Guys against girls," Leah said.

Everyone nodded and Addison was secretly happy because that meant she got to stand next to Ryan.

"Are you ready to kick my ass," he said when they were alone on their side.

"I'd say yes, but it's actually been years since I've played horseshoes. Now cornhole, I am great at."

"Good to know. I'll make sure to buy a set and not practice."

She laughed and handed him his shoes. "Should we practice?" she yelled across the yard.

Brandon scoffed. "Hell no. We play cold. My house, my rules."

"It's my house too." Leah hit him on the arm.

"Babe, come on. Practicing is just wrong."

"Guys," Addison shouted, "no practice is fine. Leah and I don't need practice to whip your asses."

It was all talk because, like she'd told Ryan, it had been years since she'd played.

"Big talk for someone who just admitted to not playing recently."

"Throw your shoes and we'll see who comes out on top."

Ryan grinned. "Top or bottom doesn't really matter to me." He threw his first shoe. "I like either."

She groaned. "Are all guys incapable of having a conversation without making all things a sexual innuendo?"

"When the woman they are currently in a relationship with is standing right next to them, it's hard not to think of all things related to sex."

It was her turn, so she threw her two horseshoes quickly then turned to Ryan. "Are we in a relationship?"

He blinked. "Oh, I don't know."

"It's just that you said, woman you are in a relationship with."

"We got one point," Leah yelled over to them, interrupting their conversation.

They both took a step back so that Leah and Brandon could throw the horseshoes.

"I wasn't trying to imply anything," Ryan said, his shoulders practically touching hers.

"I didn't think you were. I was just wondering if you were dating, or planning to date, other people or if it was just me?"

He turned to face her, his expression unreadable. "I'm not now nor do I plan to date anyone else. Hell, I didn't plan to date you, I just didn't have a choice. You snuck up on me, Addison."

She smiled up at him, since, without her heels, she was a good six inches shorter than him. "I'm not seeing anyone else either, and I don't want to." They stayed staring at each other, both with huge smiles on their faces, until Leah's voice broke the spell.

"Hey, lovebirds, do you think one of you could maybe add up the points?"

Ryan took a step forward and began checking the shoes. Leah looked over at her and made kissy lips, Addison mouthing the word stop.

"Guys got one point," Ryan announced.

The game went on for twenty minutes, with the guys eventually coming out on top, thanks to Ryan's ringer in the last round.

As they walked over to the fire to warm up, Ryan said, "I'm sorry I wasn't able to lose."

Rubbing her hands together to warm them up, she swiveled her head to look at him. "Funny thing...you winning had the same effect on me as you losing."

She knew what saying the words meant, knew that it wasn't fair to lead him on when she had no intention of sleeping with him. The longer she could hold out the better she'd feel about her skill level.

She wasn't sure what she would do if when they did finally have sex, he decided she was horrible, and didn't want to be with her any longer.

So, she was going to do her damnedest not to let that happen.

And that meant she needed help. And maybe coaching.

Chapter 7

Ryan wasn't sure how people went days on end without seeing the person they were in a relationship with. He'd had colleagues in Baltimore that would go a week or more without seeing their girlfriends and here he was dying after only three days.

He didn't know what that meant, or how he was supposed to deal with it. Should he call and beg to see her, or should he wait for her to call him?

When he'd taken her home on Saturday, after they'd left Brandon and Leah's, she hadn't been any different. She'd let him kiss her goodnight at the door, and it wasn't a chaste kiss. It was the kind of kiss that led to more, led to sex. And, while he knew they weren't having sex—and he was okay with that—her kisses, and the way she touched him and moaned into his mouth, told him she wanted him as much as he wanted her.

Then Sunday came, and when he hadn't heard from her by the afternoon, he texted just to say hi. She answered but seemed distracted. One word answers and no details. So Monday he let it go and waited for her to get in touch with him.

Only she never did.

And here it was Tuesday night, and he was in agony over what to do. Thank God for Logan. He'd called early and asked if he wanted to join him for dinner at Gayle's to discuss the gallery. Any chance to get Addison off his mind was worth it.

Not that he wanted her off his mind. He just wanted her to want the same thing. And for her to call him.

Dammit, this was why he hated dating. You were always wondering if you did something wrong, or should have done something differently.

He found Logan at a table in the back of Gayle's already sipping on a beer.

"What's up, man?" he said when Ryan walked up to the table.

Pulling the chair out to sit down, he dropped down onto it. "Absolutely nothing."

"From your tone, I'm assuming you have woman problems?"

He gave a small laugh. "I'm pretty sure women were put on this earth to drive us crazy."

Logan tipped his beer bottle toward him. "I'm dating the queen of crazy, so trust me when I tell you, you ain't wrong."

"Helpful," Ryan said.

The waitress approached them and Ryan ordered a beer and some nachos, while Logan went with a burger and fries.

"I'm no expert on women, unless they're named Melanie, so I'm not sure if I can help, but I'll try."

He wasn't sure what he could say, or if there was really anything wrong. This was why he hated dating.

"Is it weird that I haven't heard from Addison since Sunday, and even then, it was short and vague?"

Logan leaned back casually in his chair. "Ahh the whole, playing hard to get technique. It's a classic for a reason."

"But I don't think she's playing hard to get. When I dropped her off Saturday night, it seemed like we were on the same page. Like we both were all in on being in a relationship."

"Listen, man, if there is one thing I've learned throughout the years, it's that women change their minds minute-to-minute. We can't keep up, and it's useless to even try. Just wait them out, and eventually you know them well enough to know what each expression or mood means."

"How the hell am I supposed to get to the knowing her well enough part, when she won't call me back?"

"The way I see it, you have two options. Play the game she's playing and quit calling her, or, go over to her place and see what the hell is up."

The waitress handed him the beer he'd ordered and he took a long pull from the bottle. As much as he wanted to do option two, he didn't think that was the right way to go. Neither was not contacting her. He wanted her to know that he hadn't and wouldn't give up on her.

"I'm gonna have to keep thinking. I'm not ready to do anything drastic."

Logan shrugged casually. "Your choice." He took a drink from his beer. "How's dealing with the town going?"

"Not bad. Everyone is helpful and it seems as if we're going to get all the things we need."

"I was hoping that would be the case. I don't think I can handle any more surprises." He leaned forward, his elbows on the table. "I'm not averse to hard work, but this shit is stressful."

"Before you know it, the gallery will be up and running, and life will get back to normal."

"I'm counting down the days."

Their food arrived and they both dug in. Ryan was starving, having skipped lunch because he'd gotten too busy. After a few bites, he slowed and took a drink of beer.

"Other than the gallery, what's going on with you?"

"Not a whole hell of a lot." He chewed on a french fry. "Melanie and I try for as much normal as possible, and thanks to all our family and friends," he saluted him with his beer, "we get some."

"Reed, was excited to hear that you guys were thinking about getting a dog. Somehow, he's gotten it in his head that you having a dog means he has a second dog."

Logan laughed. "That might be my fault. I told him that he could dog-sit whenever he wanted."

"I don't think you will ever lack for someone to watch a dog with Reed around. Have you picked out a dog yet?"

"Not yet. I think we might go to the animal shelter this weekend and see if we find anything that fits. Neither of us wants a puppy or all the training that comes along with owning one. An adult dog that needs a good home, and is fairly relaxed, is more our style."

He nodded. "I've never had a puppy, so while I don't know from first-hand experience how hard they are to take care of, I have a good idea." Not only had he never had a puppy he'd never even had a dog. His parents were not animal people, and they didn't see the benefit in kids having a dog; any pet, for that matter.

"Have you given any more thought to what you want to do now that you are living here?"

"A little." Which was a lie. The only thing he'd thought about since he'd moved to town was Addison. At first it was sporadic. A few times a day, maybe while he slept or while he was showering, but since the first time he'd seen her again after getting to town, it had been non-stop.

The last three days had been the worst. It was bordering on obsessive.

"I might have an idea for you," Logan said. "When I bought the building for the gallery, I also bought the building next door. The tenant was a retail store, and she and her husband moved to Florida to be close to their daughter. When I saw it was for sale, I bought it, thinking I could make sure I liked whatever went in next door to me."

"So you want to what, sell it to me?"

"Maybe. If you decide you'd want to open a practice here in Cedarville, it would be a great spot for an office."

"I don't know, man, I kind of thought that if I opened a place, I'd go over to Woodridge. A bigger population means more clients."

"And I'm sure it doesn't hurt that Addison lives there."

"I wasn't...that's not why..." He gave up. He was lying to himself if he thought he hadn't chosen Woodridge because of Addison.

"You didn't know me six months ago, but before I got my head out of my ass and realized I was in love with Melanie, I used to travel all over the world taking photos. I hated living in this town, or at least that's what I told myself. But, the instant I fell in love with her, leaving town held no appeal. I would have done anything to find a way to stay in town and be near her. So don't feel like you are doing something that every other red-blooded man wouldn't do."

He sighed and ran his hands through his hair. "Is it normal to think about a woman every second of every day?"

"There is no normal when it comes to women, but in the case of me and Melanie, I still think about her all the time. She's my world, and when we aren't together, it sucks. Even now, I'm out having a great time with you while she's at work, and yet, her face is front and center in my mind."

"It's different for you though. You guys are in love and have been together for more than a week."

"Listen, I can't tell you what's right or wrong, but I can tell you that it doesn't matter if it's been three months or three days. Love comes when it wants. We have no damn control."

He didn't bother to speak up and tell Logan that he wasn't in love with Addison. He wasn't. Yet. But, he was a self-aware kind of guy, and he knew it was only a matter of time before he was head over heels for her.

If only he knew how she felt.

After a night of sleep – more like tossing and turning – Ryan made a decision. He was going to come right out and ask Addison why she wasn't returning his texts and calls. He could handle whatever she said, and if it was over, he'd be able to move on.

It was all a giant lie. He'd never be okay if she decided she didn't want to be with him, but if lying to himself was the only way to ease his own mind, he'd do it in a heartbeat.

Coffee in hand, he sat down on the couch. The house was empty with Carly at work and Tony dropping Reed at school before he also went to work. It was just him and Max.

Thumbing his phone, he pulled up Addison's text strand. He wasn't sure if texting was the way to go, but he was a giant chicken, and texting was the easy way out.

Ryan:

I'm not sure what happened since Saturday, but if you've decided that you don't want to do this, I'll understand. I'll be devastated, but I'll understand.

After hitting send, he set his phone down and tried to enjoy his coffee. It was futile but he still tried. When only minutes later his phone dinged, he snatched it up.

Addison:

Why would you think that? I told you I was really busy for the next few days with work and that I would barely have time to breathe.

He looked back through their messages. The last thing she had said to him was that she was really busy. That was it.

Picking up his phone, he hit call on her contact.

She answered immediately.

"You never said you were busy with work," he said "I thought you were blowing me off."

"I know," she said quickly, "I was just re-reading the messages and noticed that I never explained why I was really busy, and that if you'd have texted me the same thing, I'd have come to the same conclusion you did."

He sighed into the phone. "I'm so bad at this."

"Pretty sure I'm worse." She laughed, and he got hard. Her laugh was deep and meaningful. Not giggly or at all girly.

"Tony and I had a problem at a business we cover in Columbus, and since I've been dealing with them, I wanted to take care of the problem. That meant a lot of driving back and forth, and being in Columbus during the days."

Relief washed over him and finally after three days of torture he began thinking straight again. "Did everything go okay? God, you must be exhausted."

"Exhausted would be preferable to what I am right now. I feel like I could sleep for days. And yes, everything went well, and it's all fixed."

"I should let you go so you can get some sleep."

"Any chance you'd like to have dinner tonight? I figure I might be hungry after sleeping all day."

He grinned ear-to-ear, thankful she couldn't see how happy it made him for her to want to see him. "I'd love to have dinner. And tell you what, I'll bring the food so you don't have to do anything."

"You're my hero," she said over a yawn.

"Go get some sleep and I'll see you later."

He hit the end button on his phone and leaned back against the couch. She hadn't been ignoring him or trying to avoid him. They'd just had a miscommunication, something they were both going to have to work on in the future.

With a feeling of contentment, he stood and walked up to his room. He was ready to start his day knowing he'd get to end it with Addison. There was nothing else that could be more motivating.

He was supposed to meet Alice at her house before nine so they could go over tax codes for the gallery. Logan had said that once Ryan was licensed in Ohio, he'd put him on retainer to take care of all the taxes, but even with that, Alice needed to know the basics to make sure she didn't do anything against the law.

When he pulled up to the house on the lake, a yearning for something he never knew he wanted washed over him. He wanted a home and someone to share it with. And, maybe a lake outside his bedroom window that he'd see first thing in the morning. The same lake he'd take Addison out on for a late Fall ride, and they'd make love under the stars.

Holy shit.

He'd just pictured Addison in his future.

That had to mean something. His guess had to do with a certain four-letter word that he hadn't thought he was ready to think yet.

Did he love Addison? A better question though was, did she love him? He knew he was the guy, and that women wanted the guy to say it first, but he didn't think he could. Not yet, and not unless he knew they were on the same page.

The clumsy teenager in him was too afraid he'd stumble if he tried to say it first, making her wonder what in the hell she was doing with him.

But then there was the part of him that wanted to give her everything she ever wanted, including having a guy tell her he loved her.

It was a pickle, that was for sure.

Getting out of his car, he walked up to the front porch and knocked. Alice opened the door within seconds.

"Morning," she said with a big smile on her face. Her warmth and genuine joy of life, made him wish his own mom would have been more like her.

"How's it going?" he asked as they walked inside the house. A house which was homey and comfortable and lived in. His own had been a sterile place where you were barely allowed to sit on the couches.

"Good as always. I'm ready to learn from the master." They each took a chair at the kitchen table where she had her laptop all set up, along with files and files of gallery paperwork.

"I don't know if I'm the master, but I will do my best to get you up to speed." And for three hours, that's what he did. She was a fast learner, and because she knew the town so well, there were things she knew better than he did.

She insisted on feeding him lunch when they finished, and like any other man who for years had eaten take-out or microwave meals, there was no way he could say no.

When he left, he drove down the road slowly, a sign in a yard catching his eye. It was a for sale sign, and the house it belonged to was spectacular. A large ranch with a porch that wrapped around the whole house. The yard was big, bigger than even Logan's parents' yard, and because it was a corner lot, one side backed up to trees.

Braking fast, he snapped a picture of the sign so he could call the realtor. Who'd have thought that when he'd started his day it would lead to this? He'd thought for sure that he'd end up living in Woodridge over Cedarville. But, one trip to Alice's house, and he was dreaming of living on the lake in Cedarville.

It was crazy and impromptu, and totally not like him. But, that made him want it even more. He didn't want to be the old Ryan. He wanted to be this new guy who made impulsive decisions and got the girl.

Getting the girl was a very important step.

As he drove home, he thought of the offer Logan had made to him the previous night. He could have an office right in the middle of Cedarville and live in a gorgeous house on the lake. The thing was, if he wanted both of those things—and Addison—he was going to have to start making money. He didn't want to drain his savings or overextend himself financially. That meant he needed to take the bar exam and fast. The only problem was, the next one wasn't until February, and he was pretty sure he'd missed the deadline to register. He'd look into it as soon as he got home.

But February was a long way off, and he needed to make money somehow between now and then.

Once home, he found he was still able to register for the bar, so he did. After that, he contacted the Realtor and made an appointment for the next day to look at the house. He figured the sooner the better, especially if it turned out he didn't like the house. If that happened, there would be no hurry in finding a job.

He heard the bus outside and saw Max run to the front door. Standing, he walked to the door, opened it, and watched as Max ran down the drive to meet Reed. Both dog and boy skipped and played all the way up the drive.

"Ryan, guess what?"

"What, bud?"

He bounded up on the deck. "My teacher picked next week's star student, and it's me! I have to fill out this big paper with all the things about me."

He fluffed his hair. "That's awesome!"

"Can I have a cookie," he asked as he walked into the house, Max hot on his heels.

Shutting the door, he followed Reed to the kitchen. "One cookie, and then maybe something a little healthier, like an apple."

Reed scrunched his nose. "Apples are yucky, but I like bananas."

"Then a banana it is." He let Reed pick one cookie out of the jar and then handed him a banana. "Go have a seat and I'll bring you some chocolate milk."

Reed enjoyed his after school snack while telling Ryan all the details of what was going on in the first grade. Ryan loved these afternoons he got to spend alone with Reed. He didn't mind sharing him with Carly and Tony, and hell, everyone else in town, but having him alone for a few hours a day was the reason he'd moved to Cedarville. If he'd still lived in Baltimore, he'd never have any time to spend with Reed, and that would be a huge loss.

After snacks and being brought up-to-date on the first grade, Ryan helped Reed with his small amount of homework. They both decided they should save the star student poster for when Carly and Tony could help.

Homework finished, Reed asked if he could go outside and play with Max. Ryan agreed and helped Reed with his coat and hat.

House once again quiet, Ryan watched Reed and Max run around the yard. It would be weird when he moved into his own place and Ryan wondered how Reed would take it. Would he not want to leave Carly's house? Could Ryan let him live there and not see him every night? Would Carly be okay if they split the time with him?

There were so many questions that would need to be answered. Eventually. Right now though, he had to secure all the things he needed and wanted for his future.

Picking up his phone, he texted Logan.

Ryan:

I'd like to look at the space next door to your gallery, but please, let's keep this between us. At least for now.

Logan:

Come get the keys whenever. I always have them on me.

Satisfied with the answer, he set his phone back down. He'd love to go before he went to Addison's, but he knew there wasn't really time for that. He still had to come up with something for dinner for them, shower and change before driving the twenty minutes to her apartment. He was relieved when Tony walked in the door at four-thirty.

"Does your sister like Chinese food?" he asked in lieu of a greeting.

"She does." He set his bag down and took off his coat. "There's a place in the strip by our office that is her favorite. The number forty-two is what she usually gets when we order."

"Great, thanks."

"Are you guys meeting up for dinner?"

"Yeah, I'm taking it to her so she doesn't have to cook after sleeping all day."

"That's nice of you." He looked around. "Where's Reed?"

"Up in his room playing. We did his homework and he played outside. All he has left is a star of the week poster, and I thought it might be fun for all of us to help him with it together."

"Works for me. With you gone and Carly at the studio, I think I will be bad and take Reed out for some fast food." He wasn't asking, per se, but Ryan got the impression that Tony wanted his approval.

"You know I think of you like another parent to Reed, right? You don't need to ask me before you do something."

He sat down on the chair next to the couch. "It just feels weird sometimes, if you or Carly are around and I make decisions. I don't want to step on anyone's toes."

"As far as I'm concerned, this is communal parenting. We all get a say, and unless there is something that one of us just can't live with, it's fair game. We are all doing the best we can, and there are going to be times we disagree. We'll deal with them as we go."

"The small-town life is really rubbing off on you."

"If you can't beat 'em, join 'em." They both laughed. "If it's okay with you, I'm gonna shower and then head out. I'll be home later, but probably after you're all asleep."

"Go have fun and tell Addie I expect her in the office in the morning."

"I think I'll leave that one alone," he answered as he walked up the stairs. "You can tell her yourself."

Chapter 8

Sleeping all day might not have been the best idea. She probably should have tried to stay awake and just gone to bed early. Now she was going to be awake all night and the cycle would continue for another day.

She'd woken up around four, and instead of her normal quick shower, she'd taken a long, hot bath. She wasn't normally a bath person, but the day had called for it, and it was easier to shave her legs in the bath.

Not that she had a reason to shave her legs.

At least she hoped she didn't have a reason.

Or, maybe she did hope she had a reason. Who knew at this point? She still felt so bad that she'd accidentally led him to believe that she was ignoring him the whole weekend. That had not been her intention. She'd planned to send a text with why she'd be out of touch but somehow she'd gotten sidetracked and only sent the part that said she couldn't talk.

Idiot of the highest order.

If there was a way to make a guy not want her, she'd find it.

Thankfully, he was the kind of guy that called to see what was going on. She wasn't sure what would have happened if he hadn't been that type of guy.

It wasn't long after she'd gotten out of the bath and dressed, that a knock sounded on her door.

Trying not to seem overly excited she counted to ten before opening it. All that went out the window when she got her first look at him. Holding Chinese food from her favorite place in his arms, he was wearing a fitted, wool coat with a scarf wrapped around his neck. He looked every bit the city boy she knew him to be.

Except for his face.

His face was covered in what could only be called the start of a beard. He had actual facial hair. Not just day-old stubble.

And fuck, if it wasn't sexy.

"Hey," he spoke first, his voice music to her ears after not seeing him for days.

She swallowed and licked her lips. It was taking all her willpower not to jump him right there. If he hadn't been holding food from her favorite Chinese restaurant and she wasn't starving, she might have. Instead she said, "Hey, come on in," and opened the door wider. She followed him in, and as soon as he set the bags down on her table and turned back to face her, she made her move.

Grabbing the scarf, she pulled him toward her and planted her lips on his. She was greedy and wasn't willing to wait another second to feel his skin on hers. He didn't hesitate at the touch of her lips to his and she was grateful to not be this needy alone.

Her arms were trapped between their bodies, still holding on tight to his scarf. His, though, they were around her back, inching toward her ass. If her hands were free, she'd use them to help him along. But since they weren't, she wiggled even closer to him, lifting up on her toes hoping his hands would drift lower.

And they did.

Whimpering at the contact, he took the hint and gripped her ass in both hands. She wanted nothing more than to climb this man like a fucking tree and have her way with him. But she wasn't ready yet.

Loosening her grip on his scarf, she gave him a last, lingering kiss. Breathing heavily, they stared into each other's eyes.

"I'm not sure what I did to deserve that," he finally spoke, his voice ragged, "but if you give me a minute, I'm sure I can do it again."

"Those pockets of humor that you rarely show, are one of my favorite things about you." She tried to step back but his hands didn't loosen their grip on her ass.

"You think I'm joking?" His head lowered, and again they were kissing, this time him being the instigator. His newly grown facial hair was rough and abrasive against her skin.

She loved it.

She would have stopped the kiss if she could have. But, there was no denying their attraction, and since he seemed to enjoy kissing her, who was she to pump the breaks? His hands, which were still on her ass, kneaded through her jeans causing friction to other parts of her body.

The good parts.

The parts she was dying for him to touch.

The parts she sucked at using.

He pulled back first this time. "What just happened? You were with me, and then you weren't."

Shocked that he had noticed a change in her, she dropped her eyes down. "I don't know."

She felt one of his hands leave her ass, making her want to weep, and then felt fingers under her chin, lifting her head to make eye contact with him. "Hey, what's up? Did I do something wrong?"

"No!" she cried out, holding back the tears that threatened to fall.

His expression was soft and calming. "I can't help you if you won't talk to me."

"I don't need you to help." More under control, she stepped back. "I just got into my own head for a second." She congratulated herself on not lying to him. She had gotten into her own head, he just didn't need to know about what.

He eyed her carefully and nodded. "If you're sure." He finally took his coat off. "That was some greeting."

Smiling, she reached for his coat and scarf so she could hang them by the door. "It's the," she rubbed her own chin, "new look. It's sexy in a bad boy kind of way." She remembered their conversation from their date and how he said he'd never been a bad boy.

"Yeah?" he rubbed his own fingers over the hair. "And to think, I almost shaved today."

Her back was turned as she hung his coat but his statement had her whipping around fast. "Don't." She shook her head once. "I mean, you can if you want, but I like it." She liked it so much that she was imagining what it would feel like with his head between her legs, face brushing up against the tender flesh.

"I don't mind trying it out for a little while. Less shaving is always a plus."

She walked back toward the table. "What'd you bring?" Her stomach was finally noticing the smells in the room.

"Your favorite, according to Tony."

"Oh my God, I could kiss you."

"I believe you preemptively did that."

She stuck out her tongue at him. "Don't make jokes and try to get me all hot again. I am starving."

Together they unpacked the bags of food before taking it to the couch to eat. They ate in virtual silence, mainly because she was so hungry, there was no way she could talk. When she'd eaten most of her food, she finally slowed down.

"When was the last time you ate?"

"I think yesterday around this time." She took a bite of an egg roll.

"We forgot drinks," he said and stood. "What would you like?"

"Since I've lived on coffee and pop for two days, I better go with water." She continued to eat as he grabbed the drinks.

Handing her a water, he once again sat. "Tell me about your crazy weekend?"

"It's pretty boring. The whole system went down and I had to spend most of the time searching code to find the problem. Then once I did, I had to rerun a few lines and reprogram the whole system."

"Sounds like a lot of work."

"It was. And it's the first time Tony let me be in charge of such a large problem, so I wanted to make sure I did it right."

"And did you?"

She liked how he didn't say something generic like 'of course you did' or 'you could never do it wrong'. Taking a drink of water from the bottle he'd brought her, she smiled. "I believe I did."

They continued to talk, losing the awkwardness and getting into a rhythm. He talked about Reed and the fun he'd had going to the gallery on Sunday and helping paint, and about the work he was doing for Logan. He sounded happy, and even more importantly, he looked happy.

When she yawned, he took notice. "You probably need to get more sleep. I should go."

"No don't," she reached for his arm. "I'm really not tired after sleeping all day."

He eyed her speculatively. "I guess I can stay a little longer."

The hand that she'd placed on his leg, stayed where it was, as she scooted even closer to him. Lifting her other hand, she traced his jawline under the layer of hair. His eyes watched her intently as her fingers danced over his face.

"I'm dying here." His words were low, and said almost under his breath, making it hard for her to hear.

"We can't have that, now can we." Closing the distance between them, she breathed in his scent. When she was close enough to kiss him, their lips practically touching, she stopped. "Is this better?"

"Worse," he choked out, but didn't make a move to vanish the space between their lips.

Her eyes moved down to look at his lips, and when they did, his tongue slipped out and licked his bottom one. She groaned, and before she knew it, their mouths collided. She wasn't sure who moved first and didn't give a damn. All she knew was that his mouth was touching hers, and in her world, there was nothing better.

His skilled tongue, parted her lips and, soon thereafter, invaded her mouth. The slide of it against her own was what she assumed heaven felt like. Wrapping her arms around his neck, she leaned into the kiss, forcing them both back onto the couch. Since their feet were on the floor, she was only half on top of him.

And not the half she wanted.

She felt his arms come around her body and his hands grip her ass.

No tentative Ryan this time.

Even though she was only half on him, she felt his erection pressing against her leg, and man oh man, did it make her want to climb fully on top of him.

"Addison," he murmured against her skin as his lips trailed down her neck, his facial hair rough against her skin. "We should probably stop."

Moaning, she tilted her head back to give him better access. "Just a few more minutes." His tongue licked a sensitive spot on her neck before his mouth suctioned a grip. She knew there'd be a mark, was giddy at the thought. Never in all her years had a guy cared enough to give her a hickey.

A hickey. At her age.

She didn't care if it was trashy or uncool. She couldn't wait to wake up and see it on her skin, all the while remembering how she felt when he gave it to her.

Wild, sexy and out of control.

Closing her eyes, she relished in a few more kisses. Stopping was hard, but somehow, she was able to pull away.

Sitting back up without a drop of elegance, she straightened her shirt. Her hand was itching to touch the spot on her neck where he'd left his mark, but she held herself back.

"This is going to be harder than I ever imagined," he said, sitting back up.

She couldn't stop her gaze from dropping to his lap where he was, indeed, hard. Instinctively, she licked her lips.

"You're gonna have to stop that if you want me to keep this no sex promise." There was humor laced with seriousness in his voice.

Looking back up to his face, she smiled. "You'd never break your promise. It's part of what makes you the person you are. The person I like."

"Haven't you heard, I'm turning over a new leaf, becoming a new person."

"And you want to be a person who breaks promises?" She raised an eyebrow in mock questioning.

"Probably not," he shrugged, "but the reward would be damn good."

She laughed and bit her bottom lip. "I'm starting to think you are right." She wanted it to be true. Wanted them to be combustible together. Hoped and prayed that she wasn't as horrible with him as she had previously been with other guys.

"I'm gonna go," he said and stood. "Would you want to come to dinner tomorrow night at the house? I know Reed would love to see you?"

She stood along with him. "Yes, absolutely." She loved that he invited her and that he wanted her to spend time with Reed. "I'll make my mom's famous brownies and bring them for dessert."

"Reed will love that."

She walked him to the door and watched as he donned his coat and scarf. He looked as handsome as he had when he'd first walked in the door, making it that much harder for her to let him leave. Telling him to stay was on the tip of her tongue. But she knew, deep down, that she wasn't ready.

"I'll see you tomorrow," he said, and opened the door.

Holding the edge of the door with one hand, she leaned forward just a little. "Looking forward to it."

Ryan turned back to face her, the material of his coat brushing up against her body. His heady smile pulling her in once again. "Sleep well," he said, his voice an octave lower, as his eyes searched out her lips.

It was a short kiss, no more than five seconds in length. But, that was just long enough to leave her hot and bothered when she shut the door behind him.

Each time they were together, it became harder and harder not to give in to the urge to sleep with him. Her body was beginning to demand it and that meant it was time to do something about it. Finding her phone, she texted Carly.

Addison:

I need your help but you can't tell Tony.

How embarrassing would it be if her brother found out she needed sex help.

Carly:

I need to know why before I can promise that. Anthony and I don't keep secrets from each other.

Addison:

I need sex lessons.

Carly:

Ummm...you know I'm straight right? I mean I like you and all but vagina isn't my thing.

Addison:

Not like that. I need to know what I'm doing wrong and what guys really like.

Carly:

Oh, well, that I can do. I'm off in the morning so if you want we can meet up for a few hours.

Addison:

Come to the office. Tony is on-site tomorrow, so he won't be there.

Carly ended with a thumbs-up emoji and Addison set her phone down. This had to work. It needed to. She wasn't going to be able to keep seeing him without wanting more. Wanting more was causing sleepless nights and horny days.

It was getting bad.

So bad that she was thinking about taking matters into her own hands.

Huffing out a breath, she turned off the lights and went into her bedroom. She wasn't opposed to masturbating, it was a normal thing, and considering she didn't have a man to take care of her needs, she was fine doing it herself.

Except she wasn't.

She was never able to fully let herself go. And while yes, she did have orgasms, it wasn't how everyone else explained them. She never saw a light or felt as if the Earth moved. She was afraid she was the problem and that she'd never experience the feeling of being out of control.

If she was ever going to have those feelings, Ryan was going to be the one who helped her get there.

So she went to sleep, unfulfilled and horny once again.

She was pouring herself a cup of coffee when she heard the bell over the door ding. Turning, she found Carly, walking inside.

"Your sexpert has arrived!" She spread her arms wide.

Rolling her eyes, Addison took a sip of her coffee. "I'm starting to think I made the wrong decision in asking for your help."

Removing her sunglasses, Carly put her hand on her hip. "You know I am the queen and no one has as much info as me. Even if I hadn't had sex for two years before I met Anthony."

"As long as you don't have guys running for the door as soon as they're finished, you know more than me."

"Sit," Carly said, "and tell me what you want to know."

Moving behind her desk, she sat down as Carly removed her coat and sat down in front of her. "This is all so embarrassing, and honestly, I can't believe I have to talk about it."

"There's nothing to be embarrassed about. We all have our own problems and need help sometimes. Yours just so happens to be sex." She shrugged. "I promise you, I will help you get to where you and Ryan can have wild monkey sex without him walking out afterward."

Closing her eyes, she took a cleansing breath before speaking. "Okay, so I need to know what guys like and how I was doing it wrong."

"First I need to get a rundown of these sexual experiences. Give me the play-by-play, if you will."

She slapped her hand against her forehead and groaned. "What's to tell, we got naked and he stuck it in."

She raised her eyebrows. "By stuck it in, I assume you are referring to his penis?"

"What else would I be talking about?" This was beyond embarrassing. She wanted to crawl into a hole and die.

"How the hell am I supposed to know? You said he stuck it in, there are several things he could have stuck in." She waved a hand in the air above her head. "Back on track, was there any kind of foreplay...kissing, caressing, groping, handjobs. Anything?"

She shook her head from side-to-side. "No, it was just wham bam, thank you, ma'am."

"This might be part of the problem. Sex, even if it's a one night stand, which you said they weren't, should be sexy and fun, and hell, you should want to be there."

"I did want to be there."

"Unless you've been in a relationship for a while or everyone involved is too worked up, sex should be what you are leading up to while you are making out. I've had times – too many to count with your brother – where he's so hot for me and vice versa, that we both just strip and go. But, those are mutual between us. And we are both already turned on."

"So it should always start with making out?"

"Usually. You should be hot and bothered and in the heat of the moment. That way, both of you want the same thing."

"Okay, so step one, make out. I think I can handle that." Ryan usually had her worked up as soon as he walked in a room, and the kissing only heightened her response.

"Let's talk oral sex," Carly said. "How are your skills?"

Her eyes widened and her mouth dropped open. She'd never given or received oral sex. Had never had the opportunity nor had she wanted to.

Until about a week ago.

Carly slapped both her hands on the desk in front of her. "Holy fuck! The look on your face is telling me that you have never experienced the awesomeness of oral."

She nervously swallowed. "I've never had the chance."

"This might be part of the problem. Let's go one step further. Have you ever given a hand job or been fingered?"

Again she shook her head. "I told you, after we undressed, the guy just got on top and put it in. Both times."

"I'm starting to see the problem. Have you and Ryan done anything yet?"

"We've made out."

"Was it ever horizontal?"

"Last night, I was halfway on top of him."

Carly nodded. "I'm going to give you homework. Next time you are with Ryan, you need to have a good old fashioned, dry hump or mutual hands jobs."

She felt her cheeks flush. "I don't understand? How is that going to help?"

"Addison," she leaned forward, "you have to learn about each other, but more importantly, you need to learn the dynamics of sex. It's so much more than putting the P in the V. Both parties need to be ready for sex. That means, the guy needs to be hard and you need to be wet."

She wasn't an idiot. She knew those things but, she'd also assumed they would come as sex went on.

"Another thing," Carly said, "do you know what you like?"

"I'm not sure what you are asking?"

She tapped a finger against her lip. "Do you ever... self-pleasure?"

Again her cheeks reddened. "Yes."

"So you know what makes you come and what feels good. That's great. It's going to be important as you go along. The more pleasure you take from sex, the more pleasure the guy will have."

"Really?" She'd never thought about it that way. "I thought they just wanted to get off."

"Seriously, Addison, were you raised in a convent?"

"No, I just never paid attention when girls were talking about this kind of stuff. I thought it would come naturally. Obviously I was wrong."

"When are you supposed to see Ryan again?"

"I'm coming to dinner tonight at your house."

"Okay, that won't work because Reed will be there. Here's what you do. Ride to my house with Anthony. Then after dinner, Ryan will be forced to drive you home. That's your chance to implement lesson number one."

"I don't know," Addison said. "How am I supposed to tell him I've suddenly changed my mind?"

"You don't need to tell him you've changed your mind. You still aren't ready for sex. Just tell him that you want to take it to the next level."

That could work. He wouldn't be suspicious after their make-out session the night before. "But what if I suck at it, or I touch him wrong?"

"I'm not sure you can touch a penis wrong but take your cues from him. If he's not thrusting into your hand or moaning into your mouth, change it up. His movements and vocalization will tell you everything you need to know."

She wasn't sure if she could do any of the things Carly suggested but she did know that when she was with him, she wanted to do them all and more. Maybe that was a good sign and it meant this was right. With the other guys, she was never really that interested in the sex. She'd always just done it because it was the thing to do.

Maybe she and Ryan would be better together.

She could only hope.

Chapter 9

Ryan had been busy since his head had come off the pillow. He'd met with the realtor of the house as soon as he got Reed off to school. As he'd assumed, the house was perfect. Four bedrooms, three baths, a fully finished basement, a huge yard, and the kicker, lake access. It was unbelievable that he'd come upon it when he had. The couple that owned it had just put it on the market as they had decided it was too much house for their aging bodies. They loved Cedarville but wanted a condo in the center of town where they wouldn't have anything to take care of and they'd be close to shopping and restaurants.

The price was high but not so high that he wouldn't be able to afford it. Especially if he could get his business up and running.

And that led to him going by the gallery to get the keys from Logan so he could check out the space next door.

And just like the house, it was perfect.

The space was just the right size for an office, and only a minimal amount of work would help convert it to suit his needs. Right now it was one big space with a backroom. He'd need an office built-in with the front being for a receptionist. Eventually.

It was too soon to think about hiring employees.

Dropping the key back off to Logan, he pulled him aside.

"How much do you want for the space?"

A knowing smile appeared on his face as he wiped his dirty hands on a rag. "Liked it, did ya?"

"It's a great space. Perfect for a single person office. Central in location and being next to the gallery would give me great foot traffic."

"What happened to Woodridge?"

He shrugged. "Things change."

Logan named a price. "That's what I bought it for, and for you, that's what I'd sell it for."

The number was low. Way lower than he'd expected. "Don't you want to make a profit?"

"I don't need it. I'd rather have a place next door that I know won't be a problem or become an eyesore. Plus, you're family."

Ryan was touched at the gesture. He'd never known people like the ones in Cedarville. His own parents would have tried to make a profit from him if they were selling the building. This type of family, the kind that cared and wanted to help, was new to him.

"If you're serious, I'll take it."

Logan held out his hand and Ryan shook it. "You've got yourself a deal. Since you're the lawyer, I'll let you draw up the paperwork. Just let me know when I need to sign it. Until then, why don't you keep the key and start any changes you need to make."

Still in shock from Logan's kindness, Ryan went home to get back to work. He had some gallery stuff that needed to be finished, plus he needed to start studying for the bar. He wanted to pass the first time, and since it had been a few years since he'd taken it, he needed to be prepared. Not to mention, he had a house to buy and a building renovation to plan.

His life, it seemed, had gone from dull to full of surprises in a matter of twenty-four hours.

As he worked, his mind drifted to Addison. What would she think of him buying a house and an office? Would she think he was insane or was that normal life in a small town?

He heard steps on the porch and then the front door opened, showing him Carly.

"I wasn't sure if I'd see you again today," she said. "You've been a social butterfly since you moved here and, with my crazy work schedule, we don't seem to cross paths much."

"Sorry about that."

"Don't be sorry." She took a seat at the table across from him. "I'm glad you are finding enjoyment in Cedarville. It means you'll want to stay forever."

"About that," he said. She needed to know what he was thinking for the future. "I'm buying a house and an office building."

Her eyes went wide. "Umm, what?"

He laughed. "It all happened super fast but, I found this amazing house and I just knew I had to have it, and then Logan has this empty space next to the gallery that he bought, and when he offered it to me, all the pieces of the puzzle just fell into place."

She put up a hand. "Logan bought the store next to the gallery? I saw it for sale and then all of a sudden it wasn't. Never gave much thought to who purchased it after that."

"Yeah, he said he bought it so he could handpick who went in next door to him."

"Smart." She cocked her head. "And a house? What house?"

"Do you know the Ramsey's?"

"The Ramsey's that live at the end of my aunt and uncle's road?"

"The one and the same. When I was over there yesterday, I drove by and saw the for sale sign. Only hours earlier, when I drove down the street, I was dreaming of someday living in homes just like the ones on that road."

"It's fate." She smiled.

"I think it might actually be and that's strange because I've never believed in it until now."

She stared at him with a huge smile on her face. "You're buying a house and opening a business. Both in Cedarville."

"Looks like it."

"What does Addison think of this?"

"I haven't told her yet."

Her smile faded. "Why not?"

He sighed. "I'm trying really hard to make these decisions because I want to, not because someone else wants me to, and if I told her or asked her opinion, I'm afraid I would make decisions based on what she thought."

"Are you not thinking about the future with her? Hell, that's a four-bedroom house you're buying."

"Of course I'm thinking about the future. And she's in it. I want nothing more than for her to live in that big house with me, but I feel like I need to make this choice on my own."

She studied him. "Hypothetical...what if she hates the house? What would you do?"

Leaning back in the chair, he pondered her question. He hadn't really thought that far in his thought process. He'd assumed she'd love it as much as he did. But, if it came down to the house or her...well, there was no choice.

It would always be her.

"Fuck!" he swore. How had he not thought of that?

"I see you realize the error in your thinking."

"What am I supposed to do now?"

"You talk to her, see what she thinks?"

"We haven't been together long enough for that. Have we?"

She dropped her head back. "Does it matter? Take my advice here, if you want something you have to go for it. I wasted months pushing Anthony away. Months that I would love to have spent with him."

Carly wasn't the first person to tell him that and she probably wouldn't be the last. But he wasn't sure. Not that sex was everything, but until Addison was ready to be intimate with him, he wasn't sure she was ready to talk about him buying a house and her possibly, someday, living in it with him.

"I'll leave you with that thought," Carly said and stood. "I have to get to the studio soon but first I have some laundry to do."

She walked away and left him to his thoughts. All of which were of Addison.

Under normal circumstances, that wouldn't be a bad thing, but right then and there, it was causing him pain.

In his heart.

Ryan was busy making dinner when Tony walked in. He did a double-take when he saw Addison come in immediately after him. Setting the spoon and towel down, he walked out into the living room.

"Hey."

"I hope it's okay that I'm early? I thought I would just catch a ride with Tony and then, maybe later, you could take me home?"

Her words penetrated his brain. Was she saying she wanted to be alone with him? Not that he minded. He'd gladly take her home, even if it only meant a kiss on the cheek at her door.

He took the plastic container from her hands so she could remove her coat. "Taking you home will be my pleasure."

Tony stood staring at them. "Was I this annoying when Carly and I first started dating?"

Addison broke eye contact with him. "Yes, you absolutely were. And Ryan and I aren't annoying." She slapped his arm.

He grimaced. "You kinda are." He took Addison's coat and hung it in the closet. "What's for dinner? It smells great."

"Nothing special, just a white bean chili."

"Sounds good to me," Addison said. "Where's that super-cute little boy?"

"He was upstairs," Ryan said. "Go on up and say hi. He was excited when I told him you were coming over for dinner."

Addison walked upstairs, leaving him and Tony alone.

"Sorry about the annoying crack," Tony said. "It was more for her than you. It's my job as her brother to hassle her."

Thinking of his own, now gone brother, he said, "She's lucky to have you."

"She doesn't always feel that way." He followed Ryan into the kitchen, grabbing a Coke from the fridge. "So I had an interesting conversation with Carly today." His smile was like a grinning cat.

Of course, Carly told Tony about their conversation. Ryan tried to play it cool. "Yeah, what about?" As he said it, he turned to stir the chili, but his ankle gave out and he tripped. Luckily, he grabbed onto the counter to stop himself from falling.

Same old Ryan.

"You okay, man?"

"Yeah, I'm fine." That's what he got for trying to be someone he wasn't. Cool was not part of his make-up.

"Is it true that you want to buy a house here in Cedarville?"

Stirring the pot, he turned his head to look at Tony. "Maybe. I haven't made up my mind yet."

"I, for one, think it's a great idea. Reed's two houses would be close and it would be easy to make it work. As an added bonus, then Addison can buy my house in Woodridge from me."

The spoon he was using to stir the chili, dropped from his hand and landed all the way inside the pot. "What?"

"I mentioned to Addie, a little while ago, that I was thinking of maybe seeing if you wanted to rent or buy my house since I am here all the time. She got pissy with me because she said she loved that house, and asked what if she wanted to live in it? Now I won't have to worry."

Addison wanted to live in Tony's house? What about his plans and the perfect house he wanted to buy?

Now he realized Carly had been right. He was going to have to talk to her about this, and soon. If Tony offered her his house, she would ask why he'd changed his mind, and then Tony would tell her that he was buying a house.

"Did I...say something wrong?" Tony asked.

Ryan shook his head. "No, I just didn't know that Addison was interested in your house."

Tony studied him before saying, "Oh shit! You wanted her to live with you?"

"I—I—" he stuttered out. "Not right away. I just thought that maybe, down the line, if things were still going the way they are going, that she would want to."

"I don't know how I missed that." He shook his head in self annoyance. "I won't mention anything to Addie about my house."

"It's really not a big deal. It's far down the line in our relationship."

"Keep thinking that, man." He took a sip of his Coke and walked out of the kitchen. Ryan finished cooking and began setting the table for everyone to eat. They were working with Reed on eating different and new foods, so he'd be eating the same thing as the rest of them. If after five bites, he didn't like it, he was allowed to have something else.

Amazingly, he was learning to like new things.

Addison and Reed came walking down the stairs.

"Addison played checkers with me," Reed said excitedly. "And I won."

"Oh yeah?" He looked up at Addison who was giving him a sly smile. "You must be pretty awesome to beat someone like her."

"He is." She kept her hand on his shoulder.

"Go wash up, Reed. Dinner's almost ready."

Reed rushed out of the room leaving only the two of them together. Addison took a step closer.

"I don't think you greeted me properly when I got here." Her hands were behind her back and she was swaying back and forth.

"What could I possibly have been thinking?" He cupped her chin in his hand and kissed her, light and sweet. "Someone should punish me for my error."

"Maybe I will. Later." Her eyes glinted with a promise that he hoped like hell she'd keep.

"All clean!" Reed yelled as he ran back into the room. Ryan stepped back from Addison and walked to the table.

"Then let's eat." Tony strolled back into the room and both he and Addison, joined Reed and him at the table. Everyone dug in, including Reed who decided he liked it, and shockingly, ate his whole bowl.

When dinner was over, Tony offered to clean up so Addison and Ryan could spend some time with Reed. At bedtime, Reed asked if Addison could read his nightly book and tuck him in. She readily accepted and Ryan stood at the door and watched. She was so good with him and Reed really loved having her around.

So did he for that matter.

Once the story was over and Reed was all tucked in, he and Addison headed for her apartment. When he pulled in, she invited him up. Not being an idiot, he followed her up the stairs.

"I made a decision," said when he closed the door and they were both inside her place. "While I'd like to keep the no sex rule, what do you think about opening it up to other things?"

"Other things?" he said as he pulled off his coat and stalked toward her.

She fidgeted with the opening of her coat. "You know...other things."

"Like?" He wanted her to elaborate, wanted to make sure they were on the same page.

Not to mention, her saying anything sexual would be a huge turn on.

"You really want me to say it?" She was getting annoyed and that was almost as hot as her saying sex acts.

He reached her and slid her coat off her shoulders. "I think you have to if you want me to know where your line is."

"My line is no sex." She swallowed. "Everything else is fair game."

In that moment when the woman he was coming to love, gave herself over to him, he didn't feel like the clumsy, uncoordinated boy he once was.

He felt like a man who was being given the best gift a person could possibly receive.

Closing the last few inches between them, he pushed her dark, almost black hair, off her face. "What made you change your mind?" He wanted to know that she didn't feel pressured because of him.

"Because every night I go to bed and all I can think of is you. And every morning I wake up and wonder why I'm pushing you away when it would be so easy to pull you close." She stood up on her toes and kissed his lips. "I want more, do you?"

He answered by wrapping his arms around her, pulling her flush up against his body and kissing the living daylights out of her. She gripped his shoulders, trying to hold on as the kiss became more and more intense. He spun them so that her back was to the couch and slowly, without breaking their connection, lowered them down onto it.

Needing more, he began to explore her body with his hands and because Addison was vocal, she moaned under him.

"More," she said as his mouth trailed to her neck, finding the same sensitive spot he'd found the night before. Lifting his head just a little, he looked down to where he'd marked her. It was fading, but still there.

"It so fucking hot," he said as his fingertips traced over it. He'd had the primal urge to mark her, but had no idea the effect it would have.

"I kept it covered," she said breathily. "But every second of the day, I was aware of it and how it felt when you put it there."

His mouth found hers again in a scorching kiss. "Next time, make sure it shows." He wanted the world to know that this woman was his.

Gripping his hair in her hands, she pulled his head back hard, a challenge in her eyes. "Next time, make it more noticeable."

Fuck him.

Without an ounce of control left, his body ground into hers as he moved to the other side of her neck and sucked like his life depended on it. He wanted this to last, wanted to get to the part where she touched him and he touched her. But he was too far gone, and with her legs wrapped around his waist, her hands in his hair, and hot mouth moaning out his name, he came. In his pants. Like a friggin teenager.

He didn't have time to be embarrassed though. Because under him, she was still grinding, still moaning and still pulling hard on his hair.

He kept kissing her, and the hand that had been searching out her body, moved to cup her breast. And, when he ran his thumb back and forth over the tip through her clothes, he felt her shudder under him. And when she screamed out, he knew without a doubt that she came.

Breathing heavy, most of her body went lax. Her legs loosened their grip along with the hand in his hair. When he took in her flushed face and contented smile, he began to get hard all over again.

He'd made her look that way. Him, the guy who tripped over his own feet.

"Did that seriously just happen?" Her voice was lazy and full of wonder.

He brushed the hair off her face and looked into her deep brown eyes. "Disappointed?" He knew that hadn't been what she'd had in mind when they started.

Her smile grew. "How could I be disappointed when that was amazing. That's never happened to me before. Having an orgasm with my clothes on," she clarified.

"I can't say it's happened to me either." He'd never been as worked up as he'd just been and no one else had ever made him feel the way she had. Untangling himself from her, he sat up and scooted to the edge of the couch. His jeans were wet and with nothing else to wear, it looked like he'd be going home a sticky mess.

"Are you disappointed?" she asked shyly, taking him off guard.

"No. God no." He shook his head. "Addison, I was so turned on by you and what we were doing that I couldn't stop myself from coming in my pants."

She sat up a little but she was still mostly lying on the couch. "So essentially we are just two people with no control."

"No control when it comes to each other." He had control in everything else he did, but Addison fried his brain.

Again she smiled. "I like that. And, I liked being out of control. Maybe next time we can do it with our clothes off or at least partially off."

His already semi-hard dick began to grow. "If you don't want that time to be right now, you need to stop talking."

She looked down to where he was looking and saw what he was talking about. "Oh my."

"I'm going to go try and clean up a little." He stood and started to walk away.

"I think I have an old pair of Tony's sweats if you'd want to wear those?" She stood and walked in front of him.

Tony was bigger than him but anything would be better than what he was wearing. "Sure."

She rummaged around her room until she pulled out the sweats and handed them to him. But once she did, she didn't let go. "Would you want to…" She stopped talking and her eyes went wide like she couldn't believe what she'd almost said

"Would I want to what?" He was intrigued by what would make her freak out.

"Nevermind. Don't worry about it."

"Addison," he said. "Whatever it is, you can ask me. Don't you know…it's almost a guaranteed yes?"

Her eyes went soft. "I was going to ask if you wanted to stay over."

"Yes, I absolutely want to stay over, even if it means I have to sleep on that too small for me couch."

"You wouldn't have to sleep on the couch." Her smile was back. "But our rule still stands."

He pulled the pants from her hands. "Aye aye captain." He saluted her and walked into the bathroom.

As he cleaned himself up and changed, he couldn't stop his heart from beating faster and faster. He was going to get to sleep, in a bed, all night, with Addison Scott.

Life couldn't get much better, that was for sure.

Chapter 10

Dry humping hadn't been the original plan, but the orgasm she'd had made it so she didn't really care. She was more relaxed and more confident than ever. She still couldn't believe she asked him to stay the night.

Where had that come from?

But he said yes.

He said yes. To sleeping next to her. All night.

He wasn't running out the door.

Maybe she wasn't as bad at this as she thought.

Or maybe...he actually liked her enough to stay.

Making quick work of locking her door and turning off the lights, she was able to beat Ryan back to her room. She'd rolled down the bed covers and grabbed her own clothes so she could change as soon as he was finished.

When she heard the door click open, she walked back into the hallway. What she saw almost had her orgasming again, without being touched.

Ryan stood wearing nothing but low slung sweatpants.

His chest was bare. And magnificent.

She wanted to lick it like an ice cream on a hot summer's day.

"All finished," he said as if he weren't giving her a heart attack just standing there.

She swallowed the lump that had formed in her throat. "I'll just be a minute." She brushed past him, shivering at his touch. How the fuck was she supposed to sleep laying next to him all night. She obviously hadn't thought this through very well.

Changing fast, she also brushed her teeth before joining him back in her room.

"I texted Carly," he said, "to let her know I wouldn't be home and to make sure either she or Tony could get Reed ready for school."

Her hand went to her mouth. "Oh shit. I didn't even think of that."

"It's all good. Part of the joys of group parenting." He was sitting on her bed but not yet under the covers.

"Is it hard? Parenting with other people." She sat down on the opposite side of the bed and pulled the covers over her legs.

"Not really," He moved and did the same as she had. "Carly is amazing, as you know, and Tony loves Reed as much as we both do, so he's always willing to help. I'm just thankful to have people to lean on."

"How will it work when you don't live there anymore?"

"I'm not sure. I like living there, but I'm a grown man. I think at some point I need to get my own place. Plus Tony and Carly probably want some time alone."

"I never hear him complain," she said as she reached over and turned off her bedside lamp. "He loves Carly too much and would do anything for her."

"I get that," she heard him say in the dark. "But I know how I'd feel if that were me. I'd want to be alone with the person I loved."

In the dark she imagined that was them. Living together in a house, having Reed come whenever he wanted, making love whenever he wasn't around. It was a dream that had taken root and now she wasn't willing to give it up. She wanted it all.

Because somehow, she'd gone and fallen in love with Ryan.

"Thanks for asking me to say," he said, his voice close enough to give her goosebumps.

"I have a confession." What the hell was wrong with her? Why couldn't she control herself around him?

"Should I be scared?"

"Maybe," she said and turned to face him. There was virtually no light in her room, but once her eyes adjusted, she could just make out his facial features. "I've never slept in a bed with a guy."

"Ever?" His voice held no judgment.

"There was never anyone who meant enough." She knew what she was saying, was aware of how he'd take it.

"I feel honored to be your first." His hand found hers and their fingers entwined. "This is a big moment for you. We should mark it somehow."

She laughed. "Maybe we should have a parade."

"I was thinking more along the lines of a make-out session that involved another orgasm, but a parade would work."

She scooted closer to him. "I think I like your idea better." She searched out his lips, which in the dark was not easy. Without vision she had to rely on her other senses. His lips were soft and smooth, the hair on his face scratchy, but invigorating. The hand that held hers, was strong, yet comforting at the same time.

His other hand traveled down her torso before dipping under her t-shirt and touching her bare skin. Slowly it moved up, over her navel, over her shaking, barely existent abs, until it reached the underside of her breast.

Then he stopped.

She moved her body under his hand letting him know she wanted more. He took the hint, and in a second, his fingers grazed her nipple. She moaned into his mouth.

It was glorious. Even more so when he pinched it between his fingers.

Holy hell, where had that been all her life?

"You're so responsive," he whispered against her skin as he kissed her ear.

"Only with you," she said without thinking.

Wanting and needing him to feel what she was feeling, she disengaged her hand from his and began skimming her hands, over his abdomen and chest. He had only a small amount of hair, and for a guy with an office job who claimed to be bad at sports, he was surprisingly muscled. As his mouth nibbled at her neck and ear, she moved down to get a taste of her own. Sure, it made him have to stop what he was doing, but licking his chest was almost as good as being licked by him.

His skin tasted delicious. It was small traces of sweat mixed with soap and cologne.

She kept going, wanting to know if he responded like she did when his nipples were touched. Only she wanted to do it with her tongue and teeth.

Slowly, she darted her tongue out and skimmed it over the tip, making him inhale quickly.

"Mother fucker!" he swore. "Whatever you do, don't stop."

"Wasn't planning on it," she murmured against his skin. Taking the nipple into her mouth, she swirled her tongue around it before nipping it lightly with her teeth.

"Okay, okay, I lied. You have to stop or this is going to be faster than earlier."

She laughed, feeling brazen and confident. "So can I assume you liked that?"

He flipped them, so he was on top of her. "Like is not even close to how I felt having your mouth on me."

She felt the hard ridge of his cock pressing into her leg and it made her want to beg him to make love to her. Yes, she knew she was a big ball of contradiction, but when Ryan was on top of her, she couldn't think straight.

She felt him sit, his hands pushing her shirt up. She helped by pulling it over her head leaving her completely bare.

"Part of me wishes there was light so I could see you. But, the smart part of me realizes that if I saw you, I'd go up in flames. So this is probably better."

She lay still, barely breathing. She was afraid that if she took a breath, he'd stop what he was about to do. And she really wanted him to keep going.

Slowly, tortuously so, his hands slid up her stomach. Her body shivered from his touch and goosebumps appeared on her skin. When his palms smoothed along the underside of each breast, they both simultaneously moaned.

It excited her to think that he was just as turned on by touching her as she had been by touching him.

She felt his fingers search out her nipples, and when he used two fingers to pinch each one, her back arched off the bed.

"Oh my God!" she shouted.

He leaned his body in closer, and just when she thought he was going to kiss her, he went lower, his tongue licking around her left nipple.

"You're so fucking sexy," she heard him say, his voice muffled because it was pressed up against her breast. He alternated between breasts, never letting up. She was so hot and bothered that her hips were grinding up into his body. "Do you want more," he asked as his mouth continued to take her to heaven.

"Yes, yes," she panted out.

She didn't know what more meant, but she needed it. When she felt his hand dip into her shorts, she understood what more meant. And holy hell, was she excited for what was to come?

Confident fingers found their way into her shorts and flitted over her clit. Again she moaned, trying not to rip his hair out. She was on fire, and there was only one way that fire was going to go out.

Slipping halfway off her, he leaned on his side, giving himself better leverage. She felt a finger probe her opening before slowly, cautiously, slipping inside.

"Fuck!" he swore his face next to hers now. "You are so tight."

She was, and while she knew why, he had no idea. But, then and there, she didn't care. All she cared about was how good he was making her feel.

He searched out her mouth with his own as he pumped his finger in and out. She was panting heavily into his mouth, her body getting closer and closer to a release. With his finger still moving, his thumb rubbed over her clit, sending her over the edge.

"Oh God, oh God, oh God," she chanted, as her body rode out the orgasm.

Kisses peppered her face as his fingers slipped out of her, leaving her feeling empty.

"You are a Goddess," he whispered in her ear.

She turned her exhausted body to face him. "While I appreciate the compliment, you did all the work."

He laughed and kissed her bare shoulder. "That wasn't work. That was pure enjoyment."

In her position, she could still feel his erection pressing against her hip. Sliding a hand down his body, she tentatively cupped her fingers around him. "Is it your turn now?"

His hand covered hers and for a second pressed her harder against him before pulling them both away. "I think we've done enough for tonight, don't you?"

She searched his eyes in the dark. "Don't you want me to...take care of you?"

"More than you could possibly know," He kissed her forehead. "But you're tired and we've done a lot already. I won't die if I have to wait."

"But why wait when I'm willing?" Again she gripped him through the sweatpants, this time strong and firm.

He half groaned, half sighed. "I'm trying to do the right thing here, Addison."

"The right thing would be letting me give you the same pleasure you just gave me." Her hand moved up and down his hard cock. But she wanted more. She wanted to feel it, skin on skin. Frantically, she used both hands to force his sweats down over his ass. This time, when she gripped him in her hand, she felt his heat.

Yes, she had touched a penis before but she didn't remember it feeling anything like this. He was smooth yet firm. And big, or at least bigger than what she had known. And at the top, there was moisture which she spread around with her thumb.

His breathing sped up and one of his hands came up to grip her wrist. "Harder," his voice was strained.

Gripping him tighter, she began to naturally move her fist up and down. Each groan he gave, upped her confidence and spurred her on to make it better. She began to use a twisting motion along with the up and down. His noises became louder and louder, and each time she covered the head, he gave her a deep groan.

He seemed to like that.

So she did it more and after only a few minutes, he called out that he was coming. She kept up the pace as she felt his warm, sticky release cover her hand. As his breathing slowed, so did her movements.

She was in awe of what she'd just done. She hadn't thought, instead she'd just done what came naturally. And in doing so, she'd made a man come.

Her. Addison Scott, a woman who, literally, made men run from her horrible sexual experiences, had just made the hottest, sexiest, best man she'd ever known, come like a rocket.

Shaking her head a little, she accidentally let out a small laugh.

"Please tell me you aren't laughing at me," Ryan said. "I don't think my ego could take it."

"Oh my God, no," she said as she realized that he'd heard her. "Just a little internal 'how the hell did I get here' joke."

"I wanna hear all about that, but first do you think you could get me a towel or some tissues?"

Duh, of course he needed something to clean up with and so did she. Carefully moving to the side of her bed, she grabbed a box of tissues with her clean hand. After taking several for herself, she handed him the box.

Minutes later they were both clean and back under the covers.

He hadn't left.

Again she laughed.

"Okay, now you're just doing it on purpose."

"I'm sorry, really." Her laugh became more of a snicker. "I think I'm just overwhelmed with emotion, and for some reason, it's showing itself as laughter."

"Is being overwhelmed with emotion a good thing?" he asked cautiously.

"So good." She found his face in the dark and ran a hand down it. "I didn't expect it to be that...amazing, or perfect."

"Thanks for the vote of confidence." She knew he was joking but still felt compelled to expand.

"No, it wasn't you that I was worried about. It was me. Normally..." She had no idea how to say what she needed to say or why she even wanted to tell him. But she did. "In the past, I haven't performed up to the standards that I should have."

"I feel like you are trying to tell me something, but I have no idea what it is. My brain cells aren't all fully functioning right now thanks to you."

"That's just it. I've never made a guy not be able to think."

"I doubt that." She could hear the skepticism in his voice.

"It's true." She rolled so she was flat on her back, staring up at the ceiling. "Remember when I told you that I had never slept in bed with a guy? That wasn't because I didn't want to. It was because the only three times I've ever had sex, the guy left immediately after and never called again."

Silence settled in around her. She could hear him breathing next to her and wondered if maybe she'd said too much. Then the bed dipped and she heard the click of the lamp being turned on. Light assaulted her vision, and when her eyes finally adjusted, Ryan was sitting sideways, staring down at her.

"There is so much in that statement, that I'm not sure where to start."

She started to speak, but he shushed her.

She wanted to be appalled, but she was shockingly kinda turned on.

"Let's start with the three guy thing. Are you saying that you've only had sex three times? Like actually only three times?"

She nodded, unsure if he wanted her to speak.

His eyes flitted back and forth as if confused. "So you'd meet a guy, sleep with him, and then that was it."

"It wasn't quite like that," she finally spoke.

"Then explain."

"My first boyfriend was my freshman year in college. We dated about a month, and during that time, never went further than kissing. The night we did go further, the only thing we did was have sex. There was nothing else involved." She hoped he understood what she was saying. She really didn't want to go into details that they'd done nothing like she and Ryan had done that night. "When it was over, he claimed he had a big test the next day and needed sleep. So I left and never heard from him again."

"Jackass," he muttered, shaking his head. "What about the next guy?"

"Do you really want to hear this?" she huffed out, sitting up and leaning against the bed frame.

"I think I need to so I can understand you better."

She softened at his explanation. "Almost a year later, I met a guy I liked and thought liked me. We spent every day together for over a month. Again though, we only ever went as far as kissing. When we finally had sex it was no better than the first time. And afterward, he said he didn't think we should see each other anymore because he was looking for someone more experienced."

Ryan's eyes widened in shock. "Fucking asshole." His hand reached out and took hers. "I'd apologize for all men, but unfortunately there are bad ones out there."

She shrugged. "I was starting to think that maybe I was the problem. Two guys, two sexual experiences and they both were finished."

"I can promise you that it wasn't you." His thumb was running back and forth over her palm. "Tell me about the last guy?"

"It was basically the same. We dated, only kissed, and when we finally had sex, he said we weren't compatible."

"How long ago was that?"

She dropped her head back against the headboard. "Senior year of college."

Her eyes were closed so she had no idea of the expression on his face or what he was thinking.

"Addison," she heard him say. "Look at me?" She lifted up her head and opened her eyes. "Those guys...I don't know what their issues were, but you were not to blame for the sex being bad. I am in no way an expert. Hell, I barely have more experience than you. But I do know that sex should be a mutually pleasing event. They didn't do anything to help you along or get you in the mood. There should have been foreplay and touching. A lead-up, not just the main event."

"I'm starting to realize that now." She reached out and touched the hair at his chin. "You've made me feel more alive, more sensual, than I ever thought possible."

"You're all those things on your own. You don't need me to make you feel that way."

"I might not need you to feel them, but I like feeling them with you. I think we make each other better."

"Kinda like we're better together," he said, a huge, sexy grin on his face.

"I like that." She scooted closer to him. "Can I ask you something?"

His smile disappeared. "It's never good when someone asks that."

She rolled her eyes. "You said you barely had more experience than me. What does that mean?"

"It means, that while I dated some, and had a couple of month-long relationships, there haven't been that many people, nor was it that many times."

She felt her eyebrows raise. "How'd you get so, for lack of a better word, educated?"

He laughed. "I'm not sure that I am. I just took my cues from you, and did what felt right."

She circled a hand between them. "Everything you did was perfect. Anything more might have killed me."

"That's too bad," he said and scooted closer to her, "because I was thinking that together we have a lot more to learn."

"Oh," she tapped a finger to her lips, "I guess some experimentation would be all right." She pointed at him. "Tomorrow. Someone wore me out."

He smirked and returned to his side of the bed, leaning over and turning the lamp off. "Tomorrow seems so far away," she heard him say in the dark.

She laughed, turned her body into his, and snuggled with a man for the first time in her life.

Tomorrow was a long time away, but she was just happy there was going to be a tomorrow.

Chapter 11

When things were going as well as they were with him and Addison, you didn't rock the boat. That, at least, was what Ryan thought.

It had been a week since their first night together and each day only got better. They spent every evening together, and while Ryan didn't stay all night with her every time, because of Reed, he didn't feel like they were missing out. They were still taking it slow with the sex part of their relationship, so it wasn't that big of a deal.

It was actually better that he didn't spend the night with her, because on the nights he did, he found it hard to keep his hands to himself.

He was on his way to Brandon's house to hang with the guys while the ladies made food for Thanksgiving dinner. Normally, he'd be fine spending time with his friends, while Addison was with hers, but tonight he was worried. And, it was all his own fault.

That morning, he'd closed on the house that he'd fallen in love with. And Addison had no idea. At least not yet. But since Carly knew, and he figured Leah and Melanie knew, he was screwed. There was no way they were going to keep it a secret, especially when he hadn't told them that it was a secret.

It wasn't like he went out of his way to hide it from her. It just hadn't come up in conversation.

Yeah, that sounded stupid even to himself.

They'd gotten so close the last week, talked about everything. But for some reason, he couldn't bring himself to tell her about the house. Or the office he was opening.

What the fuck was wrong with him?

She was amazing, and each day he spent with her, he fell deeper and deeper in love.

And, no, he hadn't told her that yet. He'd basically just figured it out himself so there was no way he was ready to tell her.

Some days he wondered if he'd ever be ready. If he couldn't tell her about a house and a job, how the hell would he tell her that he loved her?

Pulling into Brandon's, he got out of his car and walked the short distance to the front of the house. The front door was open, so he just walked right in. There was no one around that he could see, but within seconds of being inside, he heard voices. Walking to the open basement door, he descended the steps and the voices got louder and louder.

What he found was Logan and Brandon battling it out in a wild game of ping pong.

"That hit the line!" Logan shouted after Brandon served the ball.

"Stop being a baby, it didn't hit the line."

"Judge," Logan said and looked over to where Tony was standing at the bar.

"I already told you two that I am not getting involved."

Ryan stepped deeper into the room, Brandon finally noticing him. "Hey, man, about time you got here. I need all the reinforcements I can get to put up with these two."

"What the hell did I do?" Tony asked, a dumbfounded look on his face. "I'm just sitting here minding my own fucking business while you idiots argue."

Brandon turned back to Ryan. "Sometimes I miss the days when Logan traveled all the time and was never around."

"I heard that," Logan said and hurled a ping pong ball at Brandon.

"Boys," Ryan said, feeling relaxed and right at home, "I'd have brought Reed with me if I wanted to hear bickering all night."

"Where is Reed?" Logan asked as he walked to the bar apparently over his squabble with Brandon.

"He's at your mom and dad's having a sleepover and helping with Thanksgiving set up."

Tony laughed. "You'd have thought it was his birthday for how excited he was to help with Thanksgiving."

Logan offered Ryan a beer and he gladly accepted. "From what we got out of him, he's never had a traditional Thanksgiving. I thought Carly was going to combust when she heard that. It took Tony hours to calm her down."

"She was angrier than I've ever seen her," Tony said. "But I was right there with her. How someone can treat a child that way is beyond me."

"It happens all the time," Brandon said. "We live in our little bubble here in Cedarville, but I've still seen things that piss me off when it comes to kids and how their parents treat them."

"I'm so glad that Reed has a home now and people who love him," Logan said. "And that is all because of you, Ryan." He saluted him with his beer.

Ryan shrugged awkwardly, not wanting the accolades for doing something that most sane, normal people would do. "Thanks," he said, not sure what else he could say.

After several beats of silence Logan changed the subject. "How's it going with the oh so lovely Addison?"

Now this was a topic he could discuss for hours. "Great. She's amazing, and honestly, I'm not sure how she even likes me."

"You don't give yourself an inch, do ya?" Brandon asked. "You've done something remarkable with Reed, and then because it was right, you uprooted your whole life for him. Add to it that, you're a nice guy, and you're a chick magnet."

"I don't want to be a chick magnet," he laughed. "Addison is all I want."

"She told our parents about you," Tony said. "That's a big deal.

Suddenly nervous, Ryan took a sip of his beer before asking, "She did?"

He nodded. "And don't be alarmed but mom wants to have you over for dinner."

Ryan had met Addison's parent's when he'd first come to town. But he'd met them as Ryan, the guy who took in an adorable six-year-old boy, not Ryan, the guy who was sleeping with their daughter.

Those two things were completely different.

He'd thought he'd see them again at Thanksgiving, but found out that they were visiting their own parents in North Carolina for the holiday.

He had a stay of execution. At least for now.

"I heard through the grapevine—the grapevine here being Katie down at the station—that you closed on a house this morning." Brandon said. "The big ranch at the end of the road my parents live on?"

He knew it was only a matter of time before everyone found out, he just hadn't expected it to be that fast. "It wasn't really a secret since both Carly and Tony knew about it. I just hadn't gotten around to telling everyone else."

"By everyone else, do you mean Addison?" Tony asked. "Because that's normally something she would tell me, and yet, she hasn't mentioned anything."

He sighed and pulled one of the bar stools out, sitting down. "I haven't told her yet." He looked Tony directly in the eyes figuring as her brother, he deserved nothing less. "Every time I started to tell her, I chickened out."

"Are you afraid she'll hate the house?" Logan asked.

"Honestly," he looked from Tony to Logan, "I have no idea why I'm afraid."

"You're afraid because you love her," Tony said. "And in loving her, you know that you just did something that she's going to take one of two ways. She's either going to think you don't care enough about her to ask her opinion, or that you're moving too fast, and she's not ready. Either way you lose."

It hit him then that Tony was right. He'd kept it from her in the beginning because he was so sure it was too fast and she'd think the same thing. But, now that he'd already purchased it, he was keeping it from her because he was worried she'd be upset that he didn't value her opinion.

And now he was fucked.

There was no way out of this that didn't make him look bad.

"Time out," Brandon said, putting up a hand. "Did you say that Carly knows? My cousin Carly, who can't keep a secret, if her life depends on it? And right now Addison is with Carly?"

He dropped his head down on the bar. "I'm fucked aren't I?"

"For what it's worth," he heard Tony say, "I think this is something you can fix. Is she going to be pissed? Yeah. But just be honest with her. Tell her why you were scared to tell her. But, most importantly, don't let her push you away. She's been happier the last month than I can ever remember, and that's because of you."

He lifted his head. "This is why I stay away from relationships. I suck at them."

Logan laughed. "News flash, bro, we all suck at them. And it only gets worse when you fall in love."

"He's not wrong," Brandon said. "Until I admitted to myself and then Leah that I loved her, I constantly felt like I was walking on eggshells."

"Look at us," Logan said, "being grown-ups and talking about relationships."

"Nobody ever said you were a grown-up," Brandon said sarcastically.

"I am about to own a business in town, that's pretty fucking grown-up."

"Here we go again," Tony said. "Ryan, save me from these idiots and come play some ping pong with me."

Ryan gave a small laugh and stood up. Taking several steps he picked up the paddle that was sitting on the table. "Thanks for the pep talk," he said, feeling better, but still unsure of his next move.

"That's what friends do," Tony said, and served him the ball.

When the night ended, Ryan said his goodbye's and got in his car. He was startled half to death when he looked right and found Addison sitting in the passenger seat.

"Holy fuck!" He jerked back, hitting his head against the window.

"I'd say I'm sorry I scared you, but I'm not sure I am." Her voice was cold and detached. Totally out of the norm for her.

Rubbing his head, he turned on the overhead light. "How'd you get here?" Her face was solemn, not at all angry like he expected.

"I had Melanie drop me off."

"I'm pretty sure I can guess why?"

Her hands fidgeted in her lap. "I'm not even sure what to say to you, Ryan." She didn't once look at him, instead, she stared at her lap.

"I didn't mean to not tell you. It just kinda happened."

"We've talked every day, Ryan. There were plenty of opportunities to tell me."

He took Tony's advice and went for broke. "I was so afraid that you'd see the house as me pressuring you."

"House?" She finally looked up, her expression one of confusion. "What house? I'm talking about the office you bought?"

Oh shit. "Carly didn't tell you about the house?"

"Uh, no, but Melanie did tell me about the building." Her eyes went wide. "Are you telling me you bought a house?" Her voice had gotten louder, more so than he'd ever heard it.

Inside the car, he was beginning to feel claustrophobic. There was no room to move, something he so badly wanted to do. "I bought a house at the end of the road that Logan and Brandon's parents live on."

"The ranch on the corner with the blue shutters?" Her voice was inquisitive which he'd take any day over anger.

He nodded.

She blinked. "I need you to go back for a minute. You bought a house, but you didn't tell me because you were afraid I'd think you were pressuring me?"

"At first, yeah." He turned to face her more directly. "I saw the house and had a vision, a vision of my future, and I just knew I had to have it."

Her voice was softer when she asked, "What was in the vision?"

"I'm not sure what I should say? It's the whole reason why I didn't tell you in the first place."

"Ryan," her voice was determined, "I need to know."

He so badly wanted to take her hand in his, but he knew that he couldn't until they talked this through. "It was you and me, together, several years in the future. We were outside watching Reed play." He swallowed. "Only he wasn't alone, he was playing with a young child. Our young child."

She didn't blink and for a second he wondered if she was breathing. "Is that it?"

He shook his head from side to side slowly. "You were pregnant again."

Eyes going wide, she finally blinked. "Do you have baby fever and just never told me?"

He laughed. "I can see how you would think that, but no. I have never, not once in all my life envisioned my own children, until that moment."

Her fingers were near her mouth and she began biting her thumbnail like she was thinking. "I came here angry and now...I don't even know what this emotion is."

It was now or never if he was going to do this. "Addison, there is so much I need to tell you. About the house and the office, but before any of that, the most important thing I need to say is that I love you." Saying it freed him. "I am in love with you." It was easier to say the second time.

There were tears in her eyes. "You can't just say that to me and expect me to forget that for weeks you've been lying to me."

"I know that and I know I fucked up. But I'll do anything to make it up to you, including selling the house if you hate it."

"Damn you," she pounded a fist against his shoulder. "Of course I don't hate the house."

He grabbed the hand that she'd used to hit him. "Please tell me I haven't messed this up?" He kissed her palm.

"I need to hear all of it," she said. "The whole story and don't leave anything out."

"Anything you want." He dropped her hand. "Would you like to come home with me and we can talk there?" He hadn't run it by Carly, but he was almost sure she wouldn't care.

"Talking is the only thing we are going to do," she warned.

"Talking only," he agreed and started the car.

They drove in silence the two miles to Carly's house. When they walked inside, they found the house silent. He knew for a fact that Tony was still at Brandon's, so his guess was that Carly just happened to go to bed early.

"Would you like to talk in my room?" he asked.

"That's probably a good idea."

Together they walked up to his room, Ryan shutting the door behind them. She was sitting on the bottom of his bed looking up at him. Her big brown eyes were hopeful.

Deciding that sitting with her on the bed was a bad idea, he pulled a chair over and sat directly in front of her instead.

"When I saw the house and had that strong reaction to it, it was like a lightbulb going off in my head. I wanted it, but more importantly, I wanted to be here, in this town, with these people. And then the next day, Logan mentioned the office space to me. It was like all the stars were aligning and everything I wanted was right within my reach."

Her face softened. "I get that, I really do. But why would you not talk to me?"

"I really was afraid you'd think I was moving too fast, and then as the days went on, it became more about the fact that I'd kept something this big from you. I knew you'd be mad so I just kept putting it off."

She pursed her lips and rubbed a hand over her face. "Is that all of it? Are there any other bombshells you need to tell me?"

"No," he shook his head, "there is nothing else." He wasn't sure if there was anything else he could or should say.

She studied him. "Did you mean what you said earlier?"

"That I love you? Absolutely." He leaned forward in his chair to get close to her. "Remember my last night in town before I took Reed back to Baltimore?" After she nodded, he kept going. "Did Carly ever mention that I took off for a few hours?"

"She did," she said cautiously.

"When I left her house, my first instinct was to come and find you. I needed to talk, needed help figuring out what I wanted. And you were who I wanted to help me figure it out."

"Why didn't you come to me?" She swallowed visibly, her eyes wide waiting for his answer.

"Because I knew that if I came to see you, I'd be a goner. Moving here would have been a gimme and I wanted to do it because I wanted it, not because I couldn't stay away from you." He laughed and shook his head. "But in the end, it didn't matter. You were why I moved here. And the fact that my brain somehow recognized that, after spending just a few days with you, is miraculous."

Her breathing had somehow gotten heavier while he talked, and now her chest was rising and falling to the same rhythm.

"Talk to me, Addison? Tell me what you're thinking?"

Quickly, she grabbed one of his hands. "I just keep thinking about the day Carly friended me on FaceBook and invited me to dinner. If she'd never done that, hell if Tony had never told her that I didn't have any friends, then we would have never met." She squeezed his hand and scooted closer to the edge of the bed. "No one, other than my family, has ever told me they love me." She licked her lips. "Can you say it again?"

He smiled. "I love you, Addison."

She closed her eyes, and because he felt like she needed it, he said it again. "I love you so much." He moved to the edge of his seat, their knees touching. Lifting her other hand in his, he kissed her knuckles. "I love you." This time she opened her eyes, tears glistening in the corners.

"I love you too."

Her words set fireworks off in his chest, and because he could no longer wait, he slammed his mouth against hers. Her lips gave under his and their mouths fought a fierce battle. Soon her hands were in his hair and he was pushing her back onto the bed.

His lips traveled to her ear and he bit it lightly with his teeth. Her moans spurred him on more, not to mention her hips grinding up into his own.

"You own me, Addison," he said against her skin, meaning every word.

"When you say things like that," she panted, "you make me believe we can make this work."

He lifted his head, looking down at her. "We can make this work. Haven't we already talked about the fact that we are better together?"

She smiled and he traced her lips with a fingertip. "Is it really that easy? Do people actually fall in love this fast?"

He rolled off her and looked up at the ceiling. "The lucky ones do."

He heard her breathing, and wondered again, if he'd gone too far too fast. Turning his head sideways he found her staring at him.

"You make me feel like I'm already lucky. But, and please don't take this the wrong way, I still want to go slow."

He lifted up on an elbow to see her better. "Slow is fine with me. Just knowing that you love me is enough." He ran a finger down her cheek feeling her shiver underneath his touch. "Do you want me to drive you home?" He knew sex, or any form of it, was not on the table for the night, but that didn't mean she couldn't stay and sleep next to him.

"My car is here."

Deflated by her words, he said. "I can walk you down."

"Or," her eyes searched his, "I could sleep here."

A slow smile crept across his face. "You're a mind reader."

"No," she said, finding his hand with hers. "I just know what makes me feel good."

Chapter 12

Waking, wrapped up in Ryan's arms, was Addison's new favorite thing. His body was warm as she snuggled in closer to him. One heavy arm was slung over her hip as his impressive morning wood pressed into her ass.

She wanted to stay there forever.

She could tell from his light, low breathing that he was still sleeping. That gave her time to replay everything that happened over and over in her head.

Her night had been going along great. It was a girls' night in the truest sense. There was music, wine and laughter, all the things you needed for a proper girls' night. The cooking and baking only added to the fun. Of course there was girl talk, and Carly, Leah, and Melanie wanted to know all about her and Ryan's sexy times.

She obliged and gave them what they wanted. It was after, as they were chatting about the gallery, that Melanie had let it slip about Ryan purchasing the building next door for an office.

Addison had frozen, her hands unable to continue cutting apples that would eventually become an apple pie. When she had turned, she saw in Carly's eyes that Melanie had let a secret out of the bag. Her mind had swum with all the reasons that Ryan would have kept something like that from her.

Never in her wildest dreams thinking that he'd profess his love to her.

Ryan loved her. Like actually loved her and wanted to be with her.

She sighed in his arms.

When he'd mentioned the house that again, he purchased without telling her, she almost fainted. She'd seen that house several times over the years, and more in the last few months. If she could have picked a house for herself, it would have been that one.

It was giant and a ranch was her favorite style. Plus it was on the lake. Her childhood dream had always been to live on a lake.

And now her boyfriend – she guessed that's what he was to her – was getting her dream.

And, if she wanted, she could have the dream with him.

But she couldn't. Or wouldn't. At least not yet.

She loved him. More than that though, she liked the person he was, and that was almost as important. But, was she ready to give up everything, everything she had built for herself for someone else?

And more importantly, was falling in love and moving in with someone this fast the right thing to do? What would people think?

When those words popped into her head she stiffened. Why did she care what people thought? Hadn't that been her problem with Ryan when they'd first met? She'd spent so many years making sure she lived by her own rules and not giving a fuck what others thought. So why now?

Huffing out a breath, she closed her eyes.

"What's wrong," she heard Ryan's voice murmur in her ear.

Deciding that honesty was the best policy, after all hadn't she just gone off because he'd kept something from her, she turned in his arms. "Do you care what people think?"

Sleepily, he squinted and yawned. "I used to. A lot. But now," he rubbed her exposed belly with his hand and she wanted to purr, "I've come to the conclusion that no one's opinion matters but yours."

"In high school I always cared, but then I went to college and reinvented myself to be a person that only did the things I wanted. Until about a month ago, when I once again started thinking about what people would think, before I did things."

He scrunched up his face. "I don't think I'm gonna like your answer, but what happened a month ago?"

She turned to face him fully. "I fell in love with a man who I'd just met and started wondering what people would think of it happening so fast."

"Addison," he said, but she stopped him.

"Until this morning." She smiled and ran her hands up his torso to his face that still sported hair. "I don't care what people think." When he pulled her closer with the hand that was on her hip she stopped him again. "That doesn't mean I'm ready for everything you want. Just because I don't care what other people think doesn't mean I'm not going to take the time I need to make decisions.

"Take all the time you want, as long as you promise to spend some of that time with me."

She let him pull her closer again and let him kiss her. Spending time with Ryan was not a hardship when his kisses alone could set her on fire.

"Can I ask you something," she said as he continued to kiss each and every part of her face and neck. Soon it would be hard to think.

"Mmmhmm," he murmured.

"Can you not decorate the house without me?" She knew what she was saying to him. Knew she was asking a lot. But that house was her dream home and, if it worked out that she would someday live there, she wanted to have a hand in decorating.

He stopped what he was doing and looked at her. A sweet smile formed on his lips. "I won't touch a thing without asking you first."

She relaxed both on the inside and the outside. "I'd love to see it when you have a chance."

"We can go now, if you want."

"Now?" she questioned.

"I closed yesterday."

Her mind started reeling, making her sit up. She turned her head back to look at him. "How did that happen so fast?"

"The Ramsey's had already cleaned out the place and moved into a condo in town. So when I was interested the day it went on the market, they accepted without a counteroffer. They just wanted it gone."

She played with the sheet at her waist. She'd thought she'd had several weeks to get used to the idea, but now she was finding out that he already owned it.

"Is this a problem?" He sat up and turned toward her.

His green eyes showed worry and there were lines near them. She smoothed the lines with her index fingers. "No. I just didn't know it was that far along."

He started to speak again, but there was a knock on the door.

"Come in," he said immediately.

Already speaking, Carly opened the door. "Hey I saw Addison's car still outside and I –" She broke off when she saw Addison. "Oh, I probably should have assumed."

"It got late and we were talking, so she just decided to stay."

Carly raised a hand. "I am not your mom, so no explanations needed." She eyed them both speculatively. "It looks like you worked things out though."

"We did," Addison answered and looked at Ryan. "We had a few communication issues, but they are all settled."

"Good." She nodded and began backing out of the room. "Tony and I are heading over early, around eleven, if you'd like to join."

She looked down at herself. "I need to go home first and change."

"Come whenever, we will be there," Carly said and shut the door again.

"That was not at all awkward," she said, falling back on the bed.

She heard him laugh and then felt his lips on her stomach. Opening her eyes, she looked down her body to where his mouth was on her skin. Just the sight of it made her body light up.

"What are you doing?"

He tilted his head so that their eyes met, his rough cheek against the smooth skin of her stomach. "Oh not much. Just checking out the scenery down here."

She laughed, her belly shaking. "I'm kinda liking this goofy side to you." In lieu of an answer, he continued his kissing, inching a little lower. She was wearing a t-shirt, one of his, which was now up around her breasts, and underwear. His mouth was as low as it could go without going underneath the underwear.

And then she felt his tongue dip under the elastic. She sucked in a breath. "Ryan, what did we say last night?"

"That was last night, this is today." There was mischief in his eyes. "I was thinking this would be a good chance for you to practice being quiet." He didn't give her time to ask why she needed to practice being quiet before his mouth went lower.

Her panties were still on, so there was only so much to do right?

Wrong. He trailed kisses down her covered pussy, her hips gyrating of their own accord. But then he shifted left and veered to her inner thigh. She was dying and wanted so much to beg him to touch her where it mattered.

When she moaned his name, he stopped. "You have to be quiet if you don't want anyone to hear you."

It was on the tip of her tongue to say fuck it, but then she remembered that one of those people was her brother.

"If you want me to be quiet," she whispered, "you better get to the good stuff."

He chuckled against her skin. "Is this the good stuff?" He kissed her inner thigh. "Or this?" He moved a little more to the center and kissed the edge of her panties. "Or maybe this?" His mouth closed over her pussy through the fabric.

She whimpered. "There. Right there."

"Shhh," he said, slipping a finger inside the edge of her panties and touching her. "Quiet or I'll stop."

She gripped his head, forcing his eyes higher. "Stop and I'll kill you."

Again he chuckled, but when his mouth touched her again, it was direct contact as he'd somehow pushed aside her panties.

And holy hell, she was in heaven.

His tongue delved deep, taking her high from almost the first touch. She writhed under him, her hands gripping the bed sheet to hold herself down. When he added a finger, she had to put a pillow over her face to muffle her moans and screams. For a man who hadn't done much dating, he sure knew how to eat pussy.

Uncoordinated, her ass.

When she came, he rode it out with his mouth, drinking her in. She was spent, afraid that she'd never be able to move again.

"You can remove the pillow now," he said, as he kissed his way up her body.

She threw the pillow aside, opening her eyes. "Remember how you said you were bad at sports? Well, if this was a sport, you'd be the national champion."

His eyes twinkled and he chuckled. "I think it has something to do with the person I was doing it to." He moved all the way up and dropped down beside her. "You did a pretty good job of keeping quiet. It may be time to move a little more public."

She laughed. "Sex in public is starting to lose its appeal to me. Now that I know how good it feels to be with you, I kinda don't want to have to worry about being quiet."

"And to think, we haven't even gotten to the actual sex yet."

She breathed deep wondering if she'd survive when they actually did have sex.

Thanksgiving was a giant, family-filled madhouse. There was an overabundance of food, including way too many desserts, and Addison tried them all. If she didn't stop eating so much, she was going to have to start working out, and that was not high on her list of enjoyable things.

Reed had a great time, and that time got even better, when at around four o'clock, a light snowfall began to fall.

"It's snowing, it's snowing!" He bellowed, his face glued to the window.

"News says we are going to get about three inches tonight," Alice said.

"I hate driving in snow," Addison said, to no one in particular.

"Me too," Leah agreed. "While we always had snow in New York, I never had to drive in it. So I am not looking forward to my first winter of driving in crappy weather."

"You live two miles from work," Carly said. "Two completely flat miles."

"Don't listen to her, baby," Brandon said. "I'll take you to work if it snows."

Leah snuggled in next to Brandon on the couch which mirrored what Logan and Melanie were doing. Even Carly was sitting on Tony's lap.

Only she and Ryan weren't being affectionate, and she wasn't sure if it was because of her, or because of him. But, she did know that she could remedy that.

Moving a few feet to the left, her thigh brushed his as she reached for his hand. He glanced at her, a smile on his face as their hands intertwined. Leaning down, he brushed his lips against hers, as the conversation continued around them.

She was oblivious to everyone else around them when Ryan's eyes were on hers. He made her feel cherished and wanted. And fucking hot.

She knew what she told him, that she wanted to continue to go slow, but it was going to be hard. Oh so hard.

"If you're going to get home before the snow gets bad, Addie, you might want to leave soon," Tony said.

"Oh," she said deflated. She wasn't ready to leave, and she definitely wasn't ready to leave Ryan.

"Or," Carly said. "You could stay over again."

"Again?" Leah asked. "Did I miss something?" She looked at Addison and Ryan.

"This is our cue to leave these kids alone," Alice said, pulling Charlie, her husband, and Mike, his brother, along with her.

"I kinda wish I was following them," Tony said, rubbing his forehead.

"What, pray tell, is going on?" Melanie asked. "Last night you were pissed, and then you stayed all night together?"

"Can I get anyone a drink?" Brandon said, starting to stand.

"Sit," Leah said, grabbing his arm and pulling him back to the couch.

"Oh my God," Addison said. "It's not a big deal. After Carly dropped me off, we talked it out and then we wanted to talk more, so I went back to Carly's with him. It got late, so instead of driving home, I stayed. End of story."

"So you guys are good?" Leah asked.

"Better than good," Ryan answered, squeezing her hand tighter in his own.

"Back to the reason this convo got started," Tony said. "It might be a good idea for you to stay and not drive back to Woodridge tonight."

She looked at Ryan. "Is that okay?"

"Nothing I'd love more." He stared into her eyes making her feel as if she were the only one in the room.

She was seconds from leaning forward to kiss him when she heard Logan say, "I think we should market this town as a place where people fall in love."

"No joke," Brandon said. "It's kind of insane how it's been happening."

Addison aborted the kiss and laughed along with everyone else. They continued to chat a while longer until Reed declared that the ground was covered with snow.

That was their cue to leave.

"Do you have the keys to your new house on you?" she asked as he pulled out of the driveway and onto the road.

"I do," he said, keeping his eyes on the road because of the snow. "Would you like to stop?"

"If you think we have time?"

In a matter of seconds he pulled into the driveway of her dream home. With the snow falling, it made it look even more picturesque. Opening her door and getting out, she stood, arms across the top of the door and stared.

"It really is beautiful," she said out loud. "It still boggles my mind that somehow you picked the one house to buy that I loved." She looked at him over the top of the car. "Why do you think that is?"

He slammed his car door and walked toward her. "We have a connection. Somehow, someway, my brain must have known."

She shut her door and met him in front of the car. "Maybe it wasn't your brain as much as your heart." She touched his coat where his heart would be.

With snow falling around them, he leaned in and kissed her. If this had been a movie, it would have been an unforgettable scene. She returned the kiss, both her hands now pressing against his chest.

"Let's go in before we freeze to death." He tucked her elbow in the crook of his arm and guided her up the porch steps.

She took it all in. The wide steps leading them up, the refinished wood and handrail, the huge custom made front door with the beautiful, decorative door knocker. She'd only ever viewed it from the road but up close...it was even better.

Unlocking the door, he stood back and let her go inside first. "There's a light switch on the left," he said, and she ran her fingers over the wall to find it. When the lights flicked on, her breath hitched.

It was the most beautiful home she'd ever seen.

Dark wood floors covered everything her eyes could see. The ceiling was vaulted, and to the left, there was a giant stone, floor to ceiling fireplace, that practically covered the whole wall. The living room gave way to a kitchen that was encircled by a huge half counter that looked like it could seat at least six.

"It's better than I thought." She turned to find him still standing just inside the door.

"It's beautiful," he said softly, his eyes glued to her.

She smiled. "I'm talking about the house."

"I'm talking about you." He took a step toward her. "The house pales in comparison."

Warmth crept over her. She'd been told a million times that she was beautiful but, when Ryan looked at her, she actually felt beautiful.

"Come," she held out her hand, "show me the rest of your house."

Together, they walked through the whole place. There were four bedrooms, each generous in size, and three full baths with the master having a huge jacuzzi tub. They didn't go outside because it was cold and snowing, but they did stand at the windows and examine the yard and surrounding areas.

The view of the lake was phenomenal, and the dock looked to be new.

"So what do you think?" he asked, turning his body to face hers.

"It's really perfect, Ryan. I still can't believe all this is yours."

"It's funny," he said. "I have all this furniture in storage from my old place but, when I look around, I realize that none of it will work in here."

"I'm sure that's not true."

He shook his head. "My furniture is cold and uncomfortable. This place needs homey pieces. Furniture people can relax on."

"So you'll get some new stuff." She looked back out the window where the snow was starting to fall faster. "We should probably leave."

"Wow, it's really coming down now," he said as he also looked out the window.

Quickly, they shut off the lights and left the house. Just as they got into the car, Ryan's phone rang.

"It's Brandon," he said before answering. "Hello."

Addison couldn't hear what Brandon was saying so she had no idea what he wanted or needed.

"Okay, that sounds good." He hit end on the phone. "Brandon said Main Street in town is closed because of a big wreck so we won't be able to get to Carly's. Everyone is going to Logan and Mel's and they're going to have a big sleepover."

"Is that what we are supposed to do?" She wasn't sure why but she was a little disappointed that she wouldn't have him, at least partly, to herself.

"It's probably the safest option."

She nodded and they headed off slowly toward Logan and Melanie's. The drive was quiet and peaceful with the snow falling all around them. She had been looking forward to a quiet night after a crazy twenty-four hours, but it looked like she was going to have to wait for that.

Chapter 13

Two days.

Forty-eight hours.

Two thousand eight hundred and eighty minutes.

That's how long Ryan had to go without getting to be alone with Addison.

He. Was. Dying.

First, there was Thanksgiving, and then the snowstorm that put them all sleeping together at Logan's. Ryan had thought, for sure, that Friday they'd get to be alone.

He'd been wrong.

Friday brought a problem with a business that Tony and Addison secured so they spent the day on-site trying to figure it out. By the time they finished, it had started snowing again, and they ended up stuck in Woodridge.

It wasn't like he hadn't had things to do. He spent most of the time with Reed and he'd even taken him to his new house to show him around. Reed was thrilled with the thought of living on the lake and didn't stop talking about it for hours.

But, now it was Saturday morning, and he was on his way to Addison's. He had no idea if she was there, or what he was even going to do, once he showed up. All he knew was that he missed her and had to see her.

The snow had finally let up, so his drive was smooth, and because it was early, there were very few people on the road. He made it in just under twenty minutes and hightailed it up the one flight of stairs, knocking swiftly on her door.

Seconds later, the door swung open.

"Oh thank God," she said and pulled him inside, her lips latching onto his before he heard the door close.

It was all hands, lips and moans as they kissed. He flipped them around and then backed her up against the door.

"I take it, my coming over is okay with you?" he said as he bumped his hips against hers.

"Five more minutes and I would have been on the road to see you," she said breathlessly.

"Missed you," he murmured into her skin as he kissed her neck.

"Missed you too," he heard her say. "Ryan," she pulled his head back by his hair, "I don't want to wait anymore."

He stilled, wanting to believe her because otherwise he might combust but he also didn't want to rush her. "We don't have to do anything you aren't ready for."

"I am ready. The reason for waiting isn't even valid anymore. I know you aren't leaving if I end up being bad at sex."

"You won't be bad at sex." He ran his hands up and down her arms. "One, because it's us and together, we are unstoppable, but the main reason is that it won't just be sex. We love each other and that already makes it better."

She lifted up on her tiptoes and kissed him. "Take me to bed, Ryan."

Leaning into the kiss, he pushed her further into the door. "We'll get there," he said when the kiss moved from her lips to her neck.

He was in no hurry to move to the bedroom, not when the thought of her naked and up against the door held a certain appeal. He took his time, tasting every inch of her that was exposed and when he'd finished with that, he lifted her shirt up and over her head only to find her bare beneath it. Wasting not even a second, he cupped her breasts, one in each hand, and dipped his mouth down to them.

"Oh shit," she cried out when his lips latched onto a nipple. Hearing her scream in pleasure made him go from semi-hard to rock hard in an instant.

He allowed his teeth to graze her nipple as he used his hand to tease her other breast. Lightly he cupped it and then feathered his fingers on the underside. Just when she couldn't take anymore, he pinched her nipple between his thumb and index finger.

Her moaning was all the encouragement he needed to keep going.

Dropping both his hands down her stomach as he kissed her neck, he pushed her yoga pants down her legs. She helped by lifting up a leg and pushing them down the rest of the way with her foot.

"You're wearing too many clothes," she said, and began clawing at his sweatshirt. He'd been in such a hurry to see her that he hadn't even worn a coat. Not the smartest idea, when it was cold and snowy, but right then he didn't give a damn.

She pulled it over his head and then proceeded to run her hands up his naked torso, up and around his shoulders, until she pressed her naked chest up against his.

"Oh hell, that feels good." He could feel her stiff peaks pressing into his skin and his own doing the same to her.

Her hands began to grab at the snap of his jeans and, not wanting to give too much too fast, he gripped her hand in his. "Not yet."

"No fair," she pouted.

"You'll thank me when this lasts longer than two minutes."

"You got somewhere to be?" She raised her eyebrows at him. "Because once is not going to be enough."

Her words stirred a fire inside him, and he kissed her fiercely. There was no more talking, only doing, and feeling. This time he let her unsnap his jeans and push them down his legs along with his boxers. And, when her hand gripped his cock in a tight fist, he let her pump it up and down.

He groaned into her mouth as her hand tortured him in the best possible way. Not to be outdone, he slipped his own hand between her legs, finding her already wet. His fingers splayed her open as he dipped one inside. When she began to move on his hand, he added a second finger to take her higher.

The room was filled with their pants and moans as they each brought the other to release. It was crazy and insane that they'd just given handjobs up against her front door when they had a perfectly good bedroom down the hallway.

"That took the edge off," she purred her head resting on the door.

He laughed. "Isn't that supposed to be my line?"

She looked at him lazily, her smile one of complete satisfaction. "And here I thought you were an equal opportunity kind of guy."

"I absolutely am." He leaned in and kissed her lips. "Ummm…" he looked down between them, "I need to go clean up."

"You go and I'll meet you in my bedroom." She swatted his ass as he walked away. "And hurry."

He rushed to the bathroom, and as fast as he could, cleaned himself up. Leaving his pants and underwear, which had both been halfway down his legs, in the bathroom, he walked back into her bedroom.

She wasn't there yet so he set the condom he'd grabbed from his wallet on the end table and sat down. As he was pulling the covers up around his waist, she walked in.

"Don't cover up on my account."

Naked, she leaned against the door jam.

And holy fuck if he wasn't hard again.

She was seductively drawing him in, and she wasn't even trying.

"I have a condom," he blurted, not even sure why he felt the need to say it.

She chuckled. "I'm glad you came prepared but," she walked to the bedside table and opened it, "so did I." She pulled out a whole box.

He raised an eyebrow. "High expectations, you have there."

"We don't have to use the whole box today." She set the box down and sat on the bed. "Maybe just two or three."

"Fuck!" he swore and pulled her on top of him. "You are so perfect." She straddled his hips, her breasts right in his face.

"Perfect," he said again.

"Stop." She slapped his shoulder, laughing.

"You really want me to stop." He'd begun fondling her breasts, her nipples puckering.

Her eyes dilated and she dropped her head back. "No," she said, already breathless.

"That's what I thought." He continued to play, loving how her skin flushed under his touch.

Her hands were in his hair, and when she forced his mouth to her chest, he had no plans to argue. It's the only place in the world he wanted to be at that moment. She was grinding down on him as his mouth took what it wanted.

"More," she panted, and that was all he needed.

Pushing her backward, he moved over top of her. "I don't want to rush you," he started, but she stopped him with a kiss.

"Put the condom on and fuck me."

He'd say he was shocked, but it was getting to be that nothing she said or did shocked him. Sitting back, he grabbed the condom and rolled it down his length.

"Hurry," she said, watching every move he made.

They were upside down on the bed, their heads facing the bottom and it made him laugh.

"Why are you laughing at a time like this?"

"I just find it comical that our first time is upside down."

She rubbed his back as he came back down on top of her. "It's unconventional, just like us."

He pushed the hair off her face. "Are you sure you're ready for this?"

A smile formed on her lips. "Oh yeah."

Slowly, because she was so tight, he pushed his way in. The noises she made as he went deeper made it hard to go slow. He wanted so badly to just push and bury himself inside her, never to leave. Inch by inch he slid in, until finally, he was seated fully inside her.

Taking a deep breath, he tried to calm himself before he lost it.

"Why are you not moving?" Her face was flushed and her eyes filled with passion.

"I just need a minute." His voice was strained.

She smiled an evil grin and he felt her hips begin to move. "Minute's over."

He had no choice but to move with her, his hips lifting to pull out and then push back in. Somehow, someway their bodies knew each other, and together they ground, pumped, and swirled their way toward release. He was so close, that he wasn't sure how much longer he'd be able to hold back when she shuddered under him. Letting himself go, he came with her, his body tightening inside hers.

Breathing heavy, Ryan stared into the eyes of the woman he loved. He was overwhelmed with emotion that of all the people in the world, she'd chosen him to be with. Him, the clumsy, awkward kid who could barely walk a straight line.

She ran a finger across his brow. "How can you think so hard after that?" Her voice was lazy and relaxed.

"I'm just relishing in the fact that somehow, in a sea of wrong people, we found each other."

"Almost like it was meant to be."

"Something like that." He kissed her nose, then each cheek, before zeroing in on her mouth. Pulling out, he stood and walked to the bathroom to dispose of the condom, and then rejoined her in bed. She was covered by the sheet, one leg hanging out.

It was sexy as hell.

"You haven't run out the door yet," she said, as he pulled her close.

He lifted his head and looked down at her. "Were you really expecting me to?"

Her eyes held uncertainty. "No, but it's hard to retrain my brain."

"I guess I'm just going to have to work harder to prove to you that I'm here to stay."

Her eyes went wide. "How are you going to do that?"

"Give me ten minutes and I'll show you."

"Ten minutes," she rolled on top of him, "I don't think so."

He was about to stop her, when she began to kiss her way down his chest. All of a sudden, his cock twitched to life, and no way in hell was he stopping her from putting her mouth on him.

A stupid man, he was not.

Hours later, they were sweaty, exhausted, and starving, but still they couldn't keep their hands off each other. He'd lost count how many times he'd come, and was shocked his dick was still functioning.

"No more," he panted and rolled to his back. "I can't take anymore."

"Oh, thank God," she said, her breathing ragged. "You're killing me."

"Me," he looked to the side, "you're the one that can't keep her hands to herself."

She laughed. "Okay, let's just call it a mutual killing."

Several minutes of silence followed and it gave Ryan time to just enjoy being next to her. He couldn't imagine this ever getting old.

"Are you as hungry as I am?" she asked, breaking the silence.

"Oh yeah."

They got dressed, or at least partially dressed, and went to the kitchen. After realizing she had no food in her apartment that didn't require cooking, they decided on pizza and placed an order. When it arrived, they ate on the couch, devouring the whole thing, and then snuggled up to watch a movie. Being the chivalrous guy he was, he let Addison pick, and thank God, she picked a comedy. There was no way he could sit through some chick flick, even though he would, if it meant making her happy.

Sometime during the movie they must have fallen asleep. He awoke at ten with her sprawled on top of him. He gently lifted her up and carried her to bed. She was so exhausted from both their acrobatics and her long night at work, she didn't even wake up. After laying her in bed, he went to lock up and find his phone, so he could let Carly know he wouldn't be home.

Ryan:

I'm still at Addison's, is everything good there?

Carly:

Yep! I'm assuming everything went well?

Ryan:

I'm not talking about this with you.

Carly:

You are no fun.

Dropping his phone, he turned off the lights and went back to Addison, who was sound asleep.

When he woke the next morning, he found himself alone in bed. Stretching, he groaned at his sore muscles. Muscles it was possible he'd never used, until last night. Kicking the covers off, he found his jeans and pulled them on, opting to stay shirtless.

He found Addison in the small kitchen, headphones on her ears, dancing. He stayed back so she wouldn't see him and just watched. Her body moved and swayed, and every once in a while, she would sing a lyric or two out loud. He was mesmerized by her confidence and beauty, and loved that she seemed happy.

That he made her happy.

When her back was turned, he approached her, and mid-hip swivel, he moved up behind her, wrapping his arm around her waist.

"Holy shit," she shouted, her head turning to look at him. Ripping the headphones from her ears she punched his shoulder. "You scared me to death."

Laughing, he removed the headphones from her hand and set them on the counter. "You were too sexy not to interrupt." Pulling the cord from her phone that was in her pocket, he hit play. Some pop song about staying in Paris rang out, and with her in his arms, he began to move.

"What are you doing?" she asked, her body stiffer than he would have liked.

"If you're going to dance, why not dance with me?" He swung her around in a circle.

She threw her head back and laughed. "This is not the kind of dancing you do to this song."

He dropped her arms. "Show me."

She crossed her arms over her chest and looked down at the floor. "I can't do that," she said bashfully.

"Hey," he said, stepping closer, "after all we've shared, it's dancing that has you being shy?"

She shrugged. "It's so...intimate."

He cocked his head to the side. "Even more of a reason to do it only for me."

"I can't," she said again, this time more vulnerable.

Seeing how uncomfortable it made her, he let it go. "You don't have to do anything you don't feel like doing. And I'll never push you."

"Thank you," she lifted her eyes to look at him.

"Why are you up so early?" He'd gotten a look at the clock on his way out of her room, and it was barely seven.

"Woke up starving and thought I'd make us breakfast." She indicated the already cooked bacon and pancake batter.

"Wow, an all-day sex marathon and breakfast," he joked, "you really are a goddess."

Her sultry laugh went straight to his dick, which he'd have thought needed more rest after yesterday. "I am no goddess."

"I'll be the judge of that." Again, he wrapped his arms around her, and this time nuzzled her neck.

"None of that if you want breakfast."

"What if I want you for breakfast?"

She turned in his arms. "Real food first, and then, maybe a shower together."

Appeased, he let her go while she finished the food. He offered to help, but she'd laughed him off. Instead he got plates and forks ready and did dishes as she finished with them.

It was easy being together like this.

And good.

He wanted it, always, but knew he had to wait her out. His only hope was that she'd be ready sooner rather than later.

Chapter 14

Addison was feeling guilty. Guilty that Ryan had spent the entire day and night with her when he had Reed to think about. He'd tried to stay longer on Sunday, but she'd insisted that he go home. He, then in turn, tried to get her to go with him, but again, she didn't feel right about it. Not with Reed in the house.

He'd protested several times, but eventually saw it her way, and went back home. She did not want to come between Reed and Ryan. The child had been through enough and deserved to have Ryan around.

It didn't matter that she loved him, couldn't. Reed had to be the priority.

Finishing up the paperwork from the emergency job on Friday, she hit save and closed out the file. Her morning had gone by fast, and somehow, it was already time for lunch. Tony's door was closed and she could see that he was on the phone, so she didn't bother him. He could get his own lunch.

Just outside the door, she ran into Carly.

"Hey," Addison said. "Having lunch with Tony?"

"I am, but I also wanted to talk to you, so I came early."

"Walk with me and we can talk."

"I want to hear all about your day and night with Ryan, but more importantly, I want to know why you sent him home yesterday?" They walked down the sidewalk toward the cafe on the corner.

Addison stopped walking. "He told you that?"

"No," Carly said, "but I'm not an idiot, and when he came home looking deflated and sad, I put two and two together."

She sighed and began walking again. "He needs to worry about spending time with Reed, not spending time with me."

"Hey dummy, in case you haven't noticed, he is spending time with Reed. But, and this is something I had to get used to too, there are two of us. Hell, three if you count Anthony, and I absolutely do. That's three people to share the load, and you know what, it could be four, if you stopped being an idiot."

They were standing in front of the cafe, but they didn't go in, even though it was freezing. "What if Reed gets attached and then Ryan and I break up?"

"Are you planning on breaking up with Ryan?"

The question was so absurd that it threw her off. "No, why would I?"

Carly laughed, but it wasn't out of humor, it was one of those 'you are an idiot' laughs. "You just said what if you break up?"

"I meant, what if he breaks up with me?"

"Holy hell!" She threw up her hands. "Hasn't he proved to you that he's in this? What more does he have to do?"

"People fall in love all the time, get married, have kids and still it doesn't work out. So how can I believe this is different?"

Carly half-rolled her eyes and then pulled her into the cafe. Finding a table in the corner, she practically pushed Addison into a chair. "Okay, here's the deal. Love is a gamble that you either have to take, or else be lonely forever. You know my story and why I wasn't willing to let myself love Anthony at first. But then I realized – with the help of Leah and Mel – that if I didn't give myself over to loving him fully, I'd never be happy. And they were right. I can't predict the future, but I do know that Anthony and I love each other enough to try our hardest to make it work."

She swallowed. "I pretty much get all that, but I still hate the thought of putting Reed in the middle. It would break my heart if I had any part of doing something that hurt him."

"Then don't hurt him. He's a wise boy, Addison, and he's been through a lot. What he needs is love, and he needs it from as many people as he can get it from. You being in his life is a bonus."

"So what you're saying is that I'm being a jerk and I need to get my head out of my ass."

"Pretty much."

"Was Ryan really sad last night?" She hated that she'd hurt him. or worse, made him unhappy.

"He looked like someone kicked his puppy."

"Well, fuck," she swore. "I was only trying to do the right thing."

"Piece of advice," Carly said. "There is no right thing when you're in love. Sometimes you have to go with your feelings." Carly stood. "I gotta go or else Anthony will wonder where I am."

She left and Addison didn't move. She felt like a giant ass for basically pushing him out of her apartment. It wasn't what she'd wanted, at all. She'd wanted him to stay, or more, and when he'd invited her to stay with him, she'd wanted to go, badly.

Pulling out her phone, she debated texting him, but decided against it at the last second. This was something she needed to do in person, and she had a perfect idea.

Feeling better, she ordered lunch and went back to the office to eat. Since Carly and Tony weren't there, she assumed they'd gone out, and that gave her the office to herself. As she ate, she planned in her head what she wanted to do that night.

It was simple, but it should do the trick in apologizing, and letting him know where she stood.

When Tony walked in the door, alone, thirty minutes later, she was feeling bold and brave, and it was the perfect opportunity to approach him.

"So Tony," she stood and followed him into his office. "What would you think about making me an honest to goodness office using some of the backroom space?"

He tilted his head at her. "Is that something you want?"

Rather than taking a seat, she stayed standing. "I want more than just being your assistant. I'm already doing almost half the workload, and I think I'm doing a great job."

"You are doing a great job. A fantastic job. Hell, I couldn't do this without you. If you want an office, we will make you an office." He stood. "We can get a bigger building if we need to."

"I don't think we need a bigger building, and honestly, that would only cost us more money. But, we could cut out a small portion of the lobby and some of the backroom, and voila, an office for me!"

"Get some bids from contractors and keep me in the loop." He came around his desk and stood right in front of her. "I couldn't do this without you, Addie, so whatever you need to feel like you belong, is fine by me."

She lifted up on her toes and hugged him. "I know I'm a pain, and that when you opened this place you didn't plan on sharing it with me," she stepped back, "but I love it. It challenges me and I wouldn't want to be doing anything else."

"Most days, I'm not sure what I'd do without you."

"You're never going to have to find out." She took another step back. "I'll get back to work."

"Hey Addie," he said as she walked to the door, "what did you do to Ryan?"

She didn't even bother to turn and look at him. "Something stupid, but don't worry, I'm fixing it tonight."

She walked out of his office and back to her desk with a small hop in her step. Tony had surprised her with his approval of her having her own office. She hadn't known what to expect, but an instant yes hadn't been it. Having him realize how valuable she was, made her want to jump up and down. She'd meant it when she told him she loved working there. It hadn't been her dream job, but only because she hadn't known what she wanted to do at all. Now that she was doing security, it was more fulfilling than she had ever imagined.

At the end of the day, she headed for home where she would begin implementing *Operation: forgive me, I was an idiot*. She ran around her apartment like a madman, gathering all the things she'd need, and throwing them into a bag. Satisfied she had everything, she threw the bag in her car and pointed herself toward Cedarville.

Ryan wasn't going to know what hit him.

Or, so she'd thought.

When she pulled up she didn't see his car, and when she knocked, no one answered. Pulling out her phone, she texted Leah because she knew she could answer.

Addison:

Do you happen to know where Ryan is? I thought he'd be home with Reed, but he's not here.

Leah:

Reed is here at the studio and Ryan is at Gayle's with Brandon.

"Fuck!" she swore out loud.

Leah:

Do you need the code to get in? I can give it to you.

Did she want to go in and wait for him? Is that something she should even do?

Addison:

Send it to me, but I'm not sure what I'm doing yet. Do me a favor, don't mention this to anyone.

Walking back to her car, she got in and slammed the door behind her. Of course, her plan was going to shit. That was the way of the world. At least the world she lived in.

Deciding she could either wallow in her misfortune or start over, she got going on a new plan. This time though, she was going to need help. Starting her car, she drove to the dance studio.

Running inside, she found Leah perched at her desk.

"I need a huge favor."

"Hello to you too."

She rolled her eyes. "No time for chit chat. Either you're helping or you're not."

Elbows on the desk, she rested her chin in her hands. "Hit me."

"Anyway you know that I could get the key to Ryan's new house?"

"I thought this was going to be challenging." She stood, walking deep into the office, out of sight. Seconds later, she returned holding up a key.

"What the hell?" She took the key from Leah's hand.

"Ryan gave a copy to Carly, so she could take a tour, when she had free time."

Addison looked at the key in her hand and then back to Leah. "Maybe the universe isn't conspiring against me."

She laughed. "I think whatever you have up your sleeve is going to knock Ryan's socks off."

Gripping the key, Addison grinned. "You bet it is." She practically ran out of the studio, yelling goodbye to Leah as she went. Jogging down the street, she ran into a specialty store and bought all the candles she could find, and a couple of blankets. Then she went two doors down to the camping store and bought an air mattress.

If she was gonna knock his socks off, she was going to need candles and something to sleep on.

Throwing the bags in the backseat of her car, she drove as fast as the speed limit allowed, to Ryan's new home. Letting herself in with the key Leah had given her, she flipped on the lights.

She made two more trips to the car, bringing in her own bag and all her purchases. She unpacked the mattress and plugged it in to blow it up. Once finished, she placed it in the center of the room and covered it with one of the blankets. Next, she placed the candles all around the room. She didn't light them though. That would be the last thing she did.

Grabbing her own bag, she went into the bathroom and changed into a very sexy, very skimpy, bra and thong set. They weren't comfortable and she almost never wore them, but for Ryan, she'd wear them every day if he wanted her to.

Throwing a sweatshirt on over top, to keep herself warm, she walked around the living room, lighting each of the candles, and when the last one was lit, she sent Ryan a text.

Addison:

I know I was an ass, but I want to make it up to you. Meet me at your new house ASAP.

Apologizing sucked and Addison knew that even though she'd texted it, she was going to have to say it in person at some point.

Ryan:

I can't right now, Addison.

O-kay, she hadn't expected that.

Addison:

Please. I know asking you to leave was wrong. I'm still learning how this whole thing works.

Ryan:

You hurt me. And yeah, I know I hurt you by not telling you about the house but after the day and night we shared together, how could you think it was just okay to shove me out the door?

She wanted to throw her phone across the room. Yes, she'd done a shitty thing, but he was supposed to love her, and that meant forgiving her. Searching the room, she found her gym shoes and pulled them on as she blew out all the candles. When she was finished she grabbed her coat and keys and ran out the door.

Like a bat out of hell, she drove to Gayle's. She was parked and storming inside before she realized what she was doing. She spotted Ryan and Brandon at the bar and stomped right up to them.

"What in the actual fuck, Ryan." It wasn't quite a yell, but she wasn't whispering either.

"Umm, hey, Addison," Brandon said, but she wasn't paying any attention to him. Her eyes were on Ryan.

He was giving her a strange look, but she didn't care. She'd gone there to find out what the deal was and that's what she was going to do.

"You don't get to say you love me one minute and then the next not want to talk to me."

"Addison –"

"I made love to you," that time she did whisper, "and you know how big of a deal that was for me."

"Addison," he said again, only this time louder as he stood and put her between him and the bar.

"What?"

He looked down between them. "What are you wearing?"

"That has nothing to do with –" she trailed off, remembering that she'd only thrown a jacket and shoes on. Not pants.

And her sweatshirt and coat barely covered her ass.

Where she had on a thong.

"Oh my God!" she squealed and pulled at the hem of her sweatshirt.

"Did you actually forget to put on pants?" he asked, eyebrows raised.

"I was busy blowing up the bed and setting out the candles, and then when I put on the lingerie, I only threw the sweatshirt on to keep warm while I lit the candles. Then you pissed me off and I totally forgot when I ran out the door." She closed her eyes and dropped her head against his chest.

She felt him wrap his arms around her. "You're wearing lingerie?"

She laughed into his chest. "Of course that's all you heard."

"I heard the rest, but my mind keeps coming back to the lingerie."

She thumped his chest with her fist. "I was trying to apologize and twice now, you've ruined it."

"Twice? What was the first one?"

"I came by Carly's, overnight bag in hand, and I was going to show you that I could stay and that I wanted to stay."

He dropped his forehead to hers. "Addison, I know you are still trying to work through all your emotions, but you hurt my feelings. We made love...several times, and then you pushed me out on my ass. Do you know how that felt?"

Oh God, she was a hypocrite. How had she not noticed that she'd basically done the same to him as all those guys done to her. "I do know how that feels. That's what happened to me all those other times, and I can't believe I did the same to you."

He searched her eyes. "I knew, deep down, that you were doing it because you were worried about Reed and me not spending time with him, but it still hurt." He brushed her cheek with the back of his hand. "Loving you might just be the death of me."

"You still do...love me that is?"

"Being angry with you is never going to change that." He kissed her lips. "I'm not going to stop loving you."

"I have one more question?" She looked around the bar. "How are we going to get me out of here without people seeing me?"

"I have you covered." Brandon appeared next to them. She'd forgotten all about him. "I went and got this out of my car." He handed her a blanket. "I figured you could wrap it around your waist."

"It's better than everyone seeing my thong."

"It's a thong?" Ryan's mouth dropped open.

She rolled her eyes. "Are you coming with me or am I going home alone?"

Brandon patted Ryan on the shoulder. "Since my friend here is not a stupid man, I'll see you guys later."

She heard his footfalls as he walked away and she looked back up at Ryan. "So?"

"I'll drive. We'll get your car tomorrow." He pushed her in front of him and followed, right on her heels, out the door. He steered her toward his car, which was on the side of the building. Before he opened the door though, he backed her into it and snaked his hand inside the blanket.

"Whatcha doing there?" she asked knowing one hundred percent what he was doing.

"I know it's only two miles," he said as his hand cupped her bare cheek, "but I'll never make it knowing what you have, or should I say don't have, on." His fingers played with the fabric at the top until it disappeared in her ass crack.

"Oh," she cooed and shivered in his arms, both from the cold, and the feel of his finger between her cheeks.

His mouth came down on her neck, and because she in no way wanted him to stop, she tilted her head and gripped his coat. "You know," she swallowed because it was getting hard to talk, "we have warmer places we could be doing this."

"But this is better," he said against her ear.

His mouth came down on hers in a scorching kiss that warmed her from the inside and made her forget all about the thirty-degree November chill. His tongue parted her lips, touching hers with a sensual intimacy. She resisted the urge to climb up his body and wrap her legs around his waist, even though that's exactly what she wanted to do.

"Ryan," she panted when he moved his mouth back to her neck, "I love you, but if you don't take me home and fuck me, I might kill you."

He pulled her away from the car and opened the door fast and hard. "Get in." He pushed her inside and slammed the door shut.

He was inside in under three seconds and starting the car. She watched as he took two deep breaths.

"Everything okay over there?" Humor laced her voice.

"Don't talk and whatever you do, don't touch me." He backed out and pulled onto the road. "My new house, right?"

She just nodded since he'd told her not to talk.

They made it to his house, without incident, and instead of waiting for him to come and open her door, they jumped out at the same time.

She followed him up the steps, and when he opened the door, she went inside.

The light was still on, and while the candles were out, you could still smell the smoke in the room.

He looked around. "You did all this?"

"I wanted to surprise you." His back was to her, so she quickly shed her coat and sweatshirt and kicked off her shoes. "I did this too." She waited for him to turn around. And, when he did, she was pleased with his reaction.

"Fuck me!"

She smiled. "No. Fuck me."

Chapter 15

Ryan wasn't sure where to look or what to do first. Addison was standing in front of him in a black lace push-up bra that barely covered her nipples, and a matching black lace thong. And while he could only see the front, he knew what the view from the back would look like.

Heaven.

He'd been so angry only an hour ago, but when she'd showed up—half-naked—to Gayle's, smoke coming out of her ears, and apologized, he'd known that he would eventually forgive her, because it was Addison, and he loved her. Even though sometimes she tested that love.

He might have to get mad at her more often though, if this was her way of apologizing.

"Are you going to just stand there?" she asked.

Slowly, he shook his head side to side. "Don't rush me. I'm enjoying the view."

"The view would be better over here."

He spun a finger in the air. "Turn around."

She pretended to pout, but then excruciatingly slowly, began to turn. He held his breath and watched as her ass came into view.

It was round, and smooth, and he wanted to sink his teeth into it.

He'd never been an ass man until he met Addison. Her's was one of a kind.

She stopped with her back to him and turned her head to look over her shoulder. "I had no idea you liked my ass so much?"

He took two giant steps and pressed his body up against hers, his hand caressing one ass cheek. "Now that you know, will you wear more things like this?"

Her lips were next to his ear due to her head being turned. "Or I could just wear nothing."

His heart stopped beating. He'd never survive knowing she was walking around bare-assed all over town.

But what a way to go.

Turning his own head, he kissed her lips. Both their heads were at odd angles, but it didn't seem to matter. He kept his hand on her ass and massaged it as they kissed. When it wasn't enough, he dropped to his knees. Addison gasped.

His nose skimmed the smooth skin on her ass as his hands held her hips steady. Looking up with only his eyes, he saw her head straining to turn further so she could watch him. Smiling up at her, he licked her skin, and then bit down.

"Ahhh!" she cried out.

He moved to her other cheek and did it again once again, making her cry out.

With his hands on her hips, he spun her body, so he was now eye level with her pussy. Gripping the material of her thong in his hand he pulled as hard as he could and ripped the material from her body. She almost lost her balance, but he steadied her with his hands.

His thumbs found their way between her legs and he used them to force her legs wider. Again he looked up and found her watching him. Eyes glued to hers, he moved in and licked her.

"Holy fuck," she groaned out.

Closing his eyes, he savored every lick and taste of her pussy, as his thumbs worked their way closer to the middle. He was gripping her legs with his fingers hard enough that he knew there'd be marks, but he was afraid she would fall if he let go.

When his thumb grazed her clit, she let out a long moan, making him keep up the pressure. Spreading her legs even wider, he drove his tongue deeper into her, using it to fuck her.

The words she was incoherently shouting and mumbling above him, spurred him on.

Fuck me, eat my pussy, take what you want.

He'd had no idea she was such a dirty talker, but holy shit, did he like it. Her words alone could probably make him come.

Slipping a finger inside her, he felt her clench around it, as she came instantly. He drank it all in, loving her taste.

"Stop, stop, stop." She patted the top of his head with her hand. "Too sensitive."

He chuckled, but he gave in and pulled back. Sitting back on his heels, he looked up at her face which held a satisfied smile. "Fuck, you are sexy."

"I can't think right now," she waved a hand in front of her body, "so don't make me."

Standing, he shucked his clothes as fast as he could and dragged her onto the air mattress. Limbs were tangled and hands went everywhere. He unsnapped her bra and began feasting on her breasts. She was still on her orgasm high, and everywhere he touched, she seemed to have heightened sensitivity.

She was moaning and squirming under his hands and mouth, making him press his dick harder into her leg. When she pushed him onto his back and slid down his body, he was too turned on to tell her to stop.

He wanted her mouth on him more than he wanted his next breath.

"Find something to hold onto," she practically purred, and then engulfed him in her mouth.

Her mouth took him to a place he didn't even know existed. She was rough when she needed to be, and gentle at other times. She'd take him right to the edge before slowing down and starting all over again. His shouts were loud, and without any furniture in the room, they echoed off the walls.

When he came, she held him deep in her mouth, swallowing every drop. He couldn't take his eyes off the sight of her as she did.

She slipped back up beside him.

"God, I love doing that."

He turned his head to look at her. "You won't see me complaining if you want to do it every day."

She laughed, and then surprised him, by jumping up. Spinning around the room, she said, "I feel incredible. You make me feel incredible, but more importantly, I feel incredible because I'm happy, for maybe the first time ever."

He turned on his side, propping himself up on his elbow to watch her. She danced around, arms wide, head thrown back.

"This really is a great house." She began strolling through the large living room, running her hands over the built-in bookshelves and the mantel. All the while, naked.

"You know what would be great in here," she said, as she came back over to the air mattress, "a big, dark, leather sectional. And, because this room is so huge, you'd still have room for some other pieces, if you wanted them."

He was having a hard time focusing on her words because her breasts were three inches from his face.

She snapped a finger in front of his face. "My eyes are up here," she said mockingly.

He grabbed her around the waist and rolled on top of her. "I know where your eyes are. They're my second favorite part of your body."

"Second. What's the first?"

He ran a hand down her side before sliding it under her ass and squeezing. "If you don't know, then, I guess I didn't do a good enough job worshiping it earlier."

She lifted her head and kissed his lips, slowly. "You did a magnificent job. Any better and I'd be dead." She eyed him quizzically. "Do you want to know my favorite part of your body?"

He bumped his hips against hers. "I have an idea."

She pursed her lips. "If you're gonna be like that, I'm not gonna tell you."

He kissed her neck, laughing. "Please," he whispered against her skin.

"If you must know, it's your hands." She lifted one with her own and brought it up between them. "I love how they feel against my skin and how easy they can make me surrender to you."

Her voice had gotten almost dreamy as she stared at his hand in her own. "Until this moment, I'd have never thought that hands could be deemed sexy, but you make them sound like they are."

"Touch me with them," she pressed his palm against her chest. "Make love to me, Ryan."

He couldn't deny her anything, ever, but this was one thing he wanted just as much as she did. "Condom," he said, hating that he'd have to move to go find his pants and dig through his wallet.

"Floor," she said and pointed right. He slid over enough to feel around and sure enough he came up with a small foil pouch.

Thank God for smart, forward-thinking women.

Holding himself up on one hand, he tore open the package with his teeth and somehow managed to roll the condom down his cock. With no warning, and no extra care, he pushed himself deep inside, Addison crying out in pleasure.

They moved together as one, the air mattress giving under their weight. It wasn't an ideal place for sex, but it was that or the hard floor. And, while the hard floor would be fine, if it was the only option, this, at least, was slightly better.

When she wrapped her legs around his back and dug her heels into his ass, he went deeper, pushing his release closer.

His mouth found her neck and he bit and sucked as he continued to move inside her. Her fingers were clawing at his back when he felt her arch up into him and come. It was too much for him, and he thrust deeply a few more times before screaming out in release.

He collapsed, exhausted onto her. He peppered her neck and ear with kisses, as his breathing returned to normal. Lifting himself just a little so that all his weight wasn't on her, he looked into her eyes. "This day started so shitty," he shook his head, "but now, I'm here with you and I can't think of anything better."

She ran her fingers through his hair. "I'm sorry I was the reason your day started so badly."

"Believe me, you made up for it." He rolled off her and sat up to remove the condom, only he had nowhere to go with it.

As if reading his mind, Addison said, "There's a box of garbage in the corner." He saw where she was pointing, and sure enough, there was the box that the air mattress had come in. He dropped the condom inside, and on the way back to the bed, he picked up a few pieces of their clothing.

"Sweatshirt." He held out the garment for her. "I'd offer you panties but I don't think these will do much good." He showed her the tattered material that he'd found on the floor.

"You owe me," she said as she slipped on the sweatshirt. He himself pulled on his boxers before lying back down next to her.

They laid in silence as seconds turned into minutes. His life was starting to turn out better than he could have ever dreamed, and it was all thanks to Addison.

The next day, Ryan couldn't stop smiling. Addison had blown his socks off the night before and he was still on a high. And sure, the day before, his bad mood was because of her too, but that didn't matter. He wasn't an idiot. He knew that couples fought, and he and Addison were no different. The big thing was going to be communication. If they could keep those lines open, everything would be okay.

Seeing Logan, he walked over to him. "Hey man, how's it going?"

"Better each day. The gallery is finished, and now all I have to do is stock it and price the pieces. It'll be ready to go before Christmas, and that means I get a small break before my world gets crazy."

Ryan looked around. "It really came together fast."

"Thanks to everyone pitching in and helping out. I can't tell you how much I appreciate all the help you've given."

Ryan shrugged. "Not like I had anything else to do."

"What's happening with that?" Logan walked around the gallery, Ryan following.

"I'm going to focus more on the house right now. I can't practice law until I pass the bar in Ohio and I can't even take the test until February."

"Sounds like you have it all worked out. When you're ready to work on the office, let me know and I'll be there to help."

"I'm sure I'll take you up on that. Until I can start earning money, I'm going to have to start watching my money. Between the house and the office, funds are low."

Logan stopped walking and looked at him. "We can push off the purchase of the office if you're low on cash. I'm not in any dire need for the money and, if it'll help you out, then I'm game."

"Are you sure? I really want the place, but I'd also like to furnish the house too."

"Consider it done," Logan patted him on the back. "We can deal with it after the New Year."

They finished the walk-thru and Ryan left to go pick up Reed. They were having a guys night at the new house with pizza and beer. Well, beer for Ryan and the rest of the guys, but milk for Reed.

He was a chatterbox, and as soon as he got in the car, talked non stop about the Christmas play and how he was picked to be an elf. His energy was contagious, and soon they were both singing Christmas songs at the top of their lungs.

At the house, they walked around outside first, before it got dark, so Reed could put in his two cents about what he wanted. Since there was already a boat dock, his mind didn't stray far from boats and jet skis. When they heard a car pull up, they walked back around front and found Brandon and Logan, with Tony pulling in right behind them.

Reed ran forward and began telling them all about the Christmas play and the elf he got to play. He didn't stop until they were finally all inside.

"I ordered pizza on the way here," Tony said.

"And I brought the drinks." Brandon had wheeled in a cooler. "So this is the place. I haven't been here since I was a kid."

"Look at all the work they've done." Logan was admiring the stone fireplace and the built-in bookcases. "This is gorgeous."

"You should see the kitchen," Ryan told them. "Brand new stainless steel appliances, granite countertops, and more cabinets than I could ever use."

"Come see it!" Reed pulled Tony's arm. "It has a long counter that goes all the way around."

Ryan let Reed show off the kitchen and then the bedrooms and bathrooms. After they'd toured the whole house, pizza arrived, and they sat down in the bare living room—bare except for the air mattress pushed into a corner—and ate. Reed ate fast and then asked if he could play on his iPad in the basement.

"Go ahead, but don't go outside."

His footsteps faded off and Ryan turned back to the group. "Everyone, mark your calendars, because he's gonna want you all at the Christmas play."

"The school has been putting on that same play for thirty years," Brandon said. "Logan over here even got to be Santa once."

Logan saluted them with his beer. "I was the best damn Santa that school has ever seen too."

"Don't tell Reed," Tony said. "He'll talk your ear off about it."

Ryan got up to grab them each another beer when he heard Logan ask, "What's with the air mattress?"

"Oh you didn't hear," Tony said. "My sweet sister used it to seduce Ryan."

Handing them each a beer, he sat back down. "Don't make it sound so sordid. She was trying to apologize."

"Her outfit at Gayle's was a pretty good apology." When both Logan and Tony looked at Brandon, he explained. "She came in like a bull in a china shop and stormed right up to Ryan wearing nothing but a sweatshirt and coat that barely, and I do mean barely, covered her ass. No pants."

"What!" Tony practically spit out his beer. "My sister walked into a bar half-naked?"

"Apparently, she was so mad at our boy over here that she forgot to put pants on over top of her seduction outfit."

Tony busted out in a fit of laughter, and for some reason, Logan and Brandon joined in.

"It wasn't that funny," he said. "Everyone could see her ass. How would you like it if your girlfriends were walking around with their asses showing?"

The laughter died down.

"Okay, so yeah, that would not be cool," Logan said. "No one sees Melanie's ass but me."

"What I want to know," Tony asked, "is how did Addie act once she found out she was half-naked?" His facial expression showed that he wanted to laugh, but he was holding it in on Ryan's behalf.

"She freaked and for good reason. Thank God for Brandon and the blanket he had in his car. At least I was able to get her out of there without anyone else seeing her."

"Should we assume from the air mattress and candles that you two made up?" Brandon asked.

"It was all just a big misunderstanding. We both jumped to conclusions when, what we should have done, is talk to each other." He looked around the room. "Does that happen to you guys?"

"All the fucking time," Tony answered. "At least in the beginning. Now that I know how Carly's mind works, I have a better handle on it."

"Same with Melanie," Logan said. "She flies off the handle about something before she talks to me and gets the real answer. Drives me insane." He laughed. "But I love her, so I've learned to deal with it."

Ryan sighed. "So what you're saying is that, because I love her, I just have to learn to deal with it?"

Nods happened all around him and soon, the laughter started back up, this time with Ryan joining in. When the laughter subsided, they cleaned up the pizza and joined Reed in the basement, where they spent the next few hours playing board games.

It was a perfect way to christen his new house.

Well...the second perfect way.

Chapter 16

"All right," Addison said as she walked into Dragonfly Dance and dropped her bag on a desk, "I'm officially clueless as to what to get Ryan for Christmas and that means you guys are up. Give me ideas?"

For two weeks she'd been to every store in her town, Cedarville, and even Columbus, and still nothing jumped out at her as a gift for Ryan. It needed to be special and important. There was no way she was just getting him a sweater or tie.

This was the man she loved. She had to do better than that.

"You still haven't bought him anything?" Leah asked.

"I can't find anything that's right, and now, I need help." She sat down next to Carly and slouched in the chair. "Help me, please."

"Okay," Mel said, "where have you looked?"

"Everywhere. I have literally been to every store in a two-hour radius."

"What about something for his house?" Carly asked.

"I'm already helping him buy stuff for the house. Plus, I want him to love everything he puts in the house."

Melanie stood. "Let's stop sitting around talking about it and let's go out and see what we can find."

"While we're out," Carly said, "you guys can help me with gifts for Reed. I've gotten him a ton of toys, but I want something special for his first Christmas with me."

They walked outside and all packed into Carly's car.

"What did you get your guys for Christmas?" Addison asked as they drove.

"I got Logan this awesome vintage camera," Mel said. "It's like the first one he had as a kid that his grandpa gave him. He talks about it all the time, and how that gift from his grandpa, was what got him interested in photography."

"Great gift," Carly said. "He really did love that damn camera. I was never allowed to touch it."

"Bran's been wanting this crazy-ass grill that's supposed to be amazing, so I went ahead and got it for him."

"What about Tony, Carly? What did you get him?"

"You guys are gonna laugh."

"What is it?" Mel asked.

"I got him a huge ass TV and an Xbox for the basement." She turned into the parking spot in front of a strip of stores. "He keeps talking about Bran and Logan's basements and how awesome they are. So I figured, why not start with the TV."

"I know he stays there every night," Leah said, "but has he officially moved in?"

They got out of the car and walked toward the first store. "Not yet, but it's only a matter of time. We've talked about it a little and he's totally fine moving to Cedarville."

"I think that's a great gift for him," Addison said. "And, I know for a fact, that he's ready to move in with you."

Carly stopped before opening the door to the store. "Seriously?"

She nodded. "All that's stopping him is you giving your go ahead."

"I say go for it," Leah said. "I love living with Brandon. Best thing I ever did, aside from moving to Cedarville."

They followed Carly into the store and immediately began shopping. An hour later, she was no closer to finding a gift than she had been when they'd started.

"This is the worst," she said when they sat down to lunch. "Why is this so hard?"

"Because you love him and want to get it right," Leah said.

"It's too stressful."

"I have a suggestion," Carly said.

"Well, don't keep me in suspense. Tell me?"

"You could move in with him."

She stopped moving, maybe even breathing. "It's too soon."

"Haven't we gone over this like six hundred times," Mel asked. "Stop worrying about it being too soon and worry about what feels right."

"You guys are spending most nights together now, right?" Leah asked.

"We are." It was the only thing she could get out because she was still stuck on the possibility of moving in with him.

"When is he moving into the house?" Mel asked.

She started to answer but Carly beat her to it. "He's hoping before Christmas. Reed really wants to have some of his Christmas there."

Leah's eyes went wide. "That could be a perfect gift. Hmm," she said, "but how would it work? Maybe show up wrapped like a present?"

"No that wouldn't work," Mel said. "He would just think she was the gift and want to unwrap her."

She listened to them continue to banter the whole time knowing exactly how she would do it if she were to do it.

"My coffee cup."

Each of the girls stared at her.

"What are you talking about?" Carly asked.

"I have this coffee cup that I drink out of every morning, and each day I stay at your house, I complain that my coffee doesn't taste the same out of any other cup. I could take the cup to his new house and leave it."

"And then he would find it," Leah said, clasping her hands together. "That's so cute."

"You've thought about it then?" Mel asked. "Living with Ryan?"

"It's pretty much all I think about, especially since I'm helping him decorate." She closed her eyes remembering all the furniture she'd helped him pick, each piece something she herself loved. "If I say I don't like something, he refuses to get it, even if he likes it."

"He wants you to love it so you'll live there with him," Carly said.

"I already love it."

"Then you should do it," Leah said. "Move in with him as a Christmas present."

She bit her fingernail, still unsure if she was ready, even though her heart told her to do it. "I'll think about it," she said to her friends.

They finished their lunch and Carly drove them back to the studio, and then she herself went back to the office. She had a contractor coming out to give her a bid on her new office and she did not want to be late.

When she arrived, Tony was at her desk, which was unusual.

"Why are you sitting out here?" She removed her coat and hung it on the rack by the door.

"My fucking computer crashed and I can't get anything to work."

"Is the network down or just your computer?" She walked up behind him.

"Just my computer. I'm ordering another one and, hopefully, it'll be here tomorrow."

"I have my laptop with me if you want to use it."

"Nah, I'm almost finished, and then I have an install." He made a few more keystrokes and then pushed back in his chair. "All done." He stood and walked around the desk. "Where have you been?"

"Shopping and lunch with the girls."

"Fun. Speaking of shopping, I'd like your opinion on something I got for Carly." He walked into his office and she followed.

Opening the drawer of his desk, she saw him pull out a small black box.

"No way!" She snatched the box from his hand and popped it open. Inside was a gorgeous, huge, square-cut, antique diamond ring. "Holy shit, Tony! This is gorgeous."

"Do you think?" He walked around and stood behind her, looking over her shoulder. "I had a hell of a time finding one I thought she'd love, and this one jumped out at me."

She turned and looked up at him. "You're really going to ask her to marry you?"

A smile formed on his face. "I absolutely am. I love her and want to spend the rest of my life with her."

She shut the box and handed it back to him. "I'm so happy for you, Tony. Carly is the best, and you two are amazing together."

"I'm thinking of asking her on Christmas Eve, before the big dinner."

She was about to speak, when the bell over the door dinged, and they both turned to see a contractor walk in. "Good luck," she said quickly, before greeting the contractor.

She spent the next hour walking around with the contractor and going over his bid. So far, he was the lowest, but she still had one more person to see. He left, and she filed the bid on her desk with the other two she already had.

Tony had already left for his install, and because she was intrigued, she went back into his office, opened the desk drawer, and pulled out the ring box. Flipping it open, she gazed at the ring snugly tucked inside.

It really was insanely gorgeous. She was no expert, but she was sure it had to be at least two karats, and that meant that he'd spared no expense. Not being able to help herself, she removed it from the box and slid it on her ring finger, holding her hand out in front of her to admire it.

The weight of what it meant to wear a ring that the person you love gave you hit her. It wasn't about jewelry or status. It was about picking that person, out of all the people in the world that you could have picked. It was about loving them so much, that you'd do anything for them. It was about being better together than you'd ever be apart.

And that's when it hit her. She wanted to live with Ryan. Hell, she wanted more than to just live with him. She wanted him to, one day, buy a ring, and show it to his friends before proposing. She wanted to wake up every day and know that he was there, or that if he wasn't, he would be. She wanted to help him, and Carly and Tony, raise Reed. And someday, she wanted her stomach to grow with a baby that was theirs.

It was funny, she thought when she finally came to terms with what she wanted, it would be hard, and she would be nervous. But she wasn't nervous. She was excited.

Looking at her finger one more time, she removed the ring and tucked it back into the box. After setting it back inside Tony's desk, she went out to her own desk and closed up shop. There was, of course, work that needed to be done, but nothing urgent that couldn't wait until the next day.

She had more immediate concerns, and one was time-sensitive, involving a piece of furniture she hated, and having it delivered before Christmas.

Later that night, she showed up at Carly's house just in time for dinner. She had spent most of the last two weeks sleeping there. A few times Ryan had slept at her apartment, but after their miscommunication, she didn't want him to think she didn't want to be with him. And she wanted to make sure that Reed knew he wasn't being neglected

Carly was still working, but Tony had cooked, something that still surprised her about her older brother. It wasn't fancy, just chicken and baked potatoes, but it was more than she'd ever expected from him.

"Hey," Ryan said, grabbing her around the waist and pulling her into him for a kiss. "I missed you."

"How was your day?" She ran her hand down the front of his shirt, just because she could.

"Not bad." He continued to hold her in his arms. "Logan is officially legally allowed to open since all the permits and inspections have been approved."

"I'm sure he was excited."

"He was." He loosened his grip on her and they walked into the kitchen. "How was your day?"

"Same as usual," she said, keeping her voice neutral. She didn't want to show too much excitement or he would see right through her.

Just then Reed came barreling down the stairs, Max hot on his heels. "Is dinner ready? I'm starving."

"Yes, you little piggy," Addison said jokingly, "Tony is all ready for us."

Dinner was always fast when Reed was involved, because he devoured his food. Afterward, Reed helped clear the table and then went back upstairs to play.

"Did Carly ever come up with something special to get him for Christmas?" Addison asked as they cleaned the kitchen.

"She did. Actually the three of us are going in on it together, and we were hoping maybe you'd like to also?"

"What is it?" She looked at Tony and then Ryan.

"We are getting him a swing set that is also a treehouse," Tony said.

"Oh wow," she exclaimed. "That's a great gift. He'll love it."

Ryan took her hand. "Would you want to go in on it with us?"

"Absolutely." She was honored they'd asked. Making that adorable boy happy was the best feeling in the world. "Are you guys buying it or building it?"

"A little of each," Tony said. "You buy it as a kit, and then you just have to put it together. We thought we would show him the brochure on Christmas and let him decide which one he wants."

"Within reason," Ryan added.

She laughed. "I'd make sure to say that because that kid dreams big."

When the kitchen was clean, she and Ryan sat and watched some TV with Tony before retreating to Ryan's room for some alone time. That was the one thing about staying with him every night; they had very little time alone together.

As soon as the door shut behind her, Ryan had her pressed up against it. "I really missed you today." He nuzzled her neck.

"You already said that." She grabbed onto his hair and held him close to her body. His tongue was doing wild and wicked things and she in no way wanted him to stop.

"It's worth repeating." His mouth trailed to hers and the kiss they shared was spectacular. Eight hours of not kissing always seemed to make them ravenous for each other. Plus, the man could fucking kiss. Soft lips, strong tongue and just a tiny bit of teeth biting down on her lip.

He destroyed her each and every time.

"I love you," she murmured, as the kiss ended and she relaxed back against the door. She smoothed his hair down from where she had been gripping it and took in his sexy looks. "God you're gorgeous."

He smiled a tiny, bashful smile, and traced her lips with his finger. "Aren't I supposed to say that to you?"

She sucked the tip of his finger into her mouth and not so gently bit down. His eyes flared with heat like they always did when she seduced him. She twirled her tongue around his finger, simulating like she was sucking his dick.

"Holy hell," he swore and closed his eyes. "You have to stop. Reed is still awake, and in about two minutes, I'm going to forget that and fuck you loudly against this door."

She let his finger slip from her mouth. "I just like teasing you."

"Someone should give you a gold medal, because you do it well." He moved to the bed, adjusting himself as he went. She opened the door like they did each night in case Reed wanted to come in, and then joined him on the bed.

Crossing her legs under her body, she leaned back. "What's on the menu tonight?" They'd gotten in the habit of picking something random and watching it on Netflix. They took turns picking, and tonight was Ryan's turn.

"I'm thinking the eighties classic, Mannequin."

"Never seen it."

He gaped at her. "Seriously? I didn't think there was anyone left that hasn't seen it."

"That just makes me special."

"Very special." He hit play and then took her hand. They watched about half before Reed came in, wanting Addison to read him his bedtime story.

He'd taken to asking her to read whenever she was there. She was almost positive that either Ryan or Carly had put him up to it, but she no longer cared. All she knew was that, for thirty minutes a night, she got to snuggle and read to the cutest kid in the world.

When his story was over, everyone came to say goodnight, just like most nights. Carly had gotten home sometime during storytime and also came to say goodnight.

Shutting the door halfway, they walked to the edge of the steps. "Did you make any decisions?"

Addison looked around quickly to make sure that Ryan couldn't hear them. "I think so."

Carly's eyes widened and she covered her mouth. "Does that mean you're gonna do it?"

Addison nodded, but that was as far as she got, because Ryan came up the steps.

"Hey, Carly," he said and then looked at Addison. "Ready to finish the movie?"

"Sure. See you tomorrow," she said to Carly.

This time Ryan did shut the door behind them. "I love Carly and Tony, but I can't wait to be in my own place." They sat back down on the bed.

"I know. I love staying here because of Reed, but I really like it when we get to stay at my place."

"Just think of all the room we'll have at the house?"

"And all the rooms we'll have to make love in."

He hit play on the remote, but before she could start watching, Ryan rolled on top of her. "Wanna skip the rest of the movie and make out?"

She ran her hand up his back. "I knew there was a reason I loved you."

He feasted on her mouth, both of them keeping their moans and groans silent. Being overheard by her brother or Reed was not high on her list of things she wanted to do in life. They never went past kissing and just a little groping until they were sure everyone was asleep, and this time was no different.

When they did finally make love, it was perfect, just like always, making her more sure that she was doing the right thing.

She fell asleep in his arms with the knowledge that, in less than two weeks, she'd be living with Ryan.

Chapter 17

It was moving day, and yet for some reason, Ryan wasn't feeling as happy or excited as he should. This was his new house. One that he'd fallen in love with on the spot. One in which he pictured his future with Addison. Only Addison wasn't ready to live with him, making Ryan wonder if he should just wait to move in until she was ready.

He wanted it to be theirs, not just his, and moving in without her made it feel like it was only his.

He didn't have that much to move since most of the furniture was all new. He did have boxes of dishes and kitchen items that he'd put into storage when he'd moved to Cedarville because he hadn't needed them.

Most of the furniture he had in storage he was planning on selling after the New Year. There were a few pieces he was taking to the new house though.

His desk, which he loved and had spent hours shopping for when he'd first started his job in Baltimore, was one. He was thinking of possibly putting it in his new office when he got it up and running, but hadn't one hundred percent decided yet.

Logan and Tony were meeting him at the storage facility to pack up, and, since Tony had a truck, there was no need to rent a bigger one. Brandon had to work, but was meeting them a few hours later, just like the girls.

Except for Addison.

She was helping from the start. In fact, she was already at the new house waiting on a furniture delivery.

Now if only he could get her to stay.

While Ryan was feeling unsure of the move, Reed was not. He was a ball of energy and kept asking questions.

"Will my bed be there today?"

"Can I sleep there tonight?"

"Can Max come to visit?"

"Yes to all those things," Ryan told him as they drove to the storage facility. He kept talking, the whole drive, and the only thing that shut him up was when they pulled up, they saw Logan and he had a **dog** sitting next to him.

"Logan got a dog!" Reed shouted and jumped out of the car.

Ryan followed him out and found him already on the ground petting the dog.

"What's his name?" Reed asked, looking up.

"He's a she, and her name is Gigi."

"You guys finally did it," Ryan said, petting Gigi's head.

"We did, but it was by accident. One of Melanie's student's found the dog on the side of the road, and after a month of looking for the owners and not finding them, we decided we'd go ahead and take her."

"That's great, man."

"I hope it's okay that I brought her. I didn't want to leave her alone yet."

"Not a problem. She can run around the backyard and, as you can see, Reed will have no problem playing with her."

They got busy loading up Tony's truck with all the things he was taking to the new house. It didn't take long since it wasn't a ton, and when they were finished, they all drove to Ryan's house. Reed, of course, had to ride with Logan so he could stay with Gigi.

Pulling up to the house, he saw Addison's car along with a moving truck from the appliance store. They were delivering his washer, dryer, and new television and surround sound. When he walked into the house, he saw they were busy setting up the TV.

"That was fast," Addison said.

"There wasn't too much to load." They both turned when they heard Reed giggle and barrel in, along with Gigi. "Meet Gigi, Logan and Mel's new dog."

"Oh wow!" She fell to her knees to pet the dog. "When did you get her?" she said to Logan who came in behind Reed.

"Last night."

"She's adorable."

"Can I take her outside?" Reed asked, eyes pleading.

"Stay in the fenced-in part," Ryan said, as he opened the back door. "I guess he no longer cares where his bed goes."

"Kids have short attention spans," Tony said, a box in his arms. "Where do you want this?"

Addison spoke before he could. "Since it says kitchen, I would assume that's where it goes." She pointed toward the kitchen.

"All boxes are marked," he added, "so just drop them in the appropriate room."

They began to unload the boxes from the truck and, when that was finished, they moved on to the few pieces of furniture he'd brought with him to put in the new house. In that time, the TV and entertainment center were all set up and running, along with the washer and dryer.

Leah and Carly showed up around eleven and began helping Addison unpack boxes. While they did that, Ryan and the guys set up the basement TV system and his computer. At one point, he was left alone downstairs and, when Logan and Tony never came back down, he went upstairs looking for them.

"Hey where'd everyone go?" he said as he walked through the doorway into the living room.

He stopped when he saw Addison.

She was sitting in the chair that he'd picked out, but she had vetoed.

More so, she was drinking out of her favorite coffee cup. The cup that she loved and said made her coffee taste better.

"What's going on?" He felt like she was trying to tell him something, but, he was sure it wasn't the thing he wanted her to be telling him.

"Oh, I'm just relaxing in this new chair and having a cup of coffee." She ran her hand down the arm of the chair.

"Where'd this chair come from?" He took a few steps into the room.

"I ordered it for you."

He scrunched up his face. "But you hated that chair in the store."

She cocked her head to the side. "I hated it, but you loved it, and that was the problem."

"I think I'm missing something."

"If this is going to be our home, it needs to be just that...ours. Not mine and not yours. You need the things you like just as much as I want things I like."

He was frozen in place, his head replaying what she'd just said over and over. "Our home?" he asked.

She set her cup on the floor and stood. Slowly, she walked toward him. "I've been shopping for two weeks trying to find the perfect Christmas present for you when it hit me, the thing you want the most and the thing that I want the most, is the same thing. So, why not make us both happy and go ahead and move in?"

"You want to live here?" He raised his eyebrow in question, still so very confused.

"Ryan, pay attention." She closed the distance between them. "I want to live here with you. I want this to be our home; a home we share together."

She was right in front of him now, the smell of violets assaulting his senses. A smell he couldn't wait to have surrounding him each and every day.

Gripping her around the waist, he pulled her against him. "Is this real?"

She smiled. "Why don't you kiss me and find out?"

He dropped his forehead to hers. "I think it's a dream."

"Not with us it isn't." Instead of waiting for him to kiss her, she sealed her lips to his. The second they touched, he knew without a doubt, that he wasn't dreaming. Addison's dream kisses were never as good as the real thing.

He started to take the kiss deeper when he remembered all the people in the house. "Where is everyone?" He glanced around but didn't see or hear any people.

"I sent them all away." A wicked smile appeared on her face.

"So they all knew what you were planning?" He brushed a stray hair from her face.

"They knew that I wanted you alone to explain how much I love you and how much I'd love to live with you."

"Thank God I fell in love with a smart woman."

"Wait until you see what I have in store for you on that chair."

He raised an eyebrow. "Something dirty, I hope?"

"Something very dirty." She walked backward and pulled him with her. When they were in front of the chair, she spun him and pushed him down. When she lowered herself to her knees in front of him, he felt himself harden.

Swiftly, her small hands began to unbutton his jeans. He couldn't take his eyes off them. It was almost mesmerizing to watch. When she pulled at his jeans, he lifted his hips to help without even thinking about it. And, when her fingers wrapped around his cock, he sucked in a deep breath.

"Addison," he breathed out.

"Welcome home." She looked up at him, a sly smile on her face before lowering her head and taking him into her mouth.

He hissed out a breath as her tongue began to tease and torture him. He wasn't sure if he was coming or going, all he knew was that he wanted this, her, for the rest of his life. She took him deeper, adding her hand at the base, to drive him even more nuts. As her head bobbed up and down, he watched intently and tried his best to hold back as long as he could. When he could no longer hold back, he tapped her head.

"Addison." His voice sounded drugged and raw even to himself.

"Addison," he said again when she kept going, not stopping for even a second.

He was out of control and past the point of no return. Whether she wanted it or not, he was going to come in her mouth.

Groaning, he emptied himself into her willing mouth, his body finally relaxing.

He kept his eyes on her as she sat back and licked her lips.

That one swipe of her tongue across her lip was the sexiest thing he'd ever seen.

"You sure do know how to give a good housewarming gift."

She was still on her knees looking up at him. "That gift was only one I'd give to you."

"Damn right." He hauled her to her feet and pulled her onto his lap. Pushing her hair off her face, he kissed her nose, then lips. "I love you so much."

She smiled and ran her hand down the side of this face. "How crazy is it that two people who have never been in relationships, found love with each other? Sometimes I still think it's a dream."

"It's no dream." He kissed her again, this time deeper and longer.

"As much as I'd love to keep doing this all day," she said, peppering kisses over his cheeks, "our friends should be back soon and you still have a couple of deliveries coming."

He sighed. "Can't we just lock out the rest of the world?"

"Tonight. When the house is all put together, it will just be you and me."

"And a six-year-old boy who has insane amounts of energy."

She laughed. "I'm sure we will be able to hold off long enough for him to go to sleep."

"Speak for yourself." Reluctantly, he let her go and she stood up. He pulled his pants back up and buttoned them. "They didn't know we were doing this, did they?"

"I didn't specifically say what we were doing, but I'm gonna go ahead and assume they know some sexual activities were going on."

Of course, they would. You couldn't get anything past those people. He reached out and pulled Addison in closer. He loved touching her and loved it even more that he could do it whenever he wanted.

"Soon, we have to get your stuff and move you in."

Her eyes gleamed. "Where do you think our friends are?" She laughed. "I've been gradually packing things up, and they went to pick it all up."

"You are amazing."

"Not really. I just knew what I wanted, and I wasn't willing to wait around to make it happen."

He kissed her and, while it started soft and slow, it soon developed into a full-blown, knock your socks off, kind of kiss. He couldn't seem to control himself when he had her in his arms. A noise outside broke them apart, and when he looked out the window, he saw that their friends were back.

"Alone time is over."

She smacked his ass. "It'll be here again before you know it."

There was a knock on the door, and then loudly, Carly yelled, "Is it safe to enter?"

Ryan shook his head and went to open the door. A smug Carly stood outside. "I'm really starting to hate you," he said with no anger behind it.

"You love me and you know it." She walked past and everyone else followed behind.

"Ignore her," Tony said, and stopped right in front of him. "Looks like you're getting yourself a roommate."

"She's so much more than that," he answered honestly.

Tony reached out his arm and gripped Ryan's shoulder. "Welcome to the family."

Family. That word meant something different now than it had the last few years. There were people in Cedarville who actually cared about him. They cared whether or not he was happy, or, if he needed help.

It was what had been missing from his life for years. And now that he had it, he never wanted to give it up.

Good thing he wouldn't have to.

Reed walked up to him, his big eyes staring up at him. "Is Addison going to live here with you?"

Ryan squatted so he was face-to-face with Reed. "Is that okay?"

"What about Carly?"

"Carly will still live at her house still and sometimes, you will stay there with her, and sometimes you will be here with me and Addison. We talked about this, remember?"

"I guess." He shrugged his small shoulders.

"Reed, hey, look at me." Ryan scooted closer. "You are what is most important. Carly and I love you, and so do Addison and Tony. But, just because Addison is going to live here too doesn't mean I love you any less."

He seemed to think about it for a minute before asking, "Can we get a dog?"

Ryan shook his head and laughed. "We can talk about it." Standing, he took Reed's hand and joined everyone else in the living room.

They spent the rest of the day, bringing in the remainder of his belongings and Addison's. The last delivery was his bed and his couch, which he'd purchased at the same store. After it was all set up, they all settled in the living room for sub sandwiches and beer.

"How's it feel to be an actual resident of Cedarville now?" Logan asked.

He looked at Addison who was sitting next to him. "Pretty damn good."

"Not only are we pulling people from other states, but we are also getting them from neighboring towns," Melanie said.

"I still live in Woodridge," Tony said.

Leah scoffed. "You sleep in Cedarville seven nights a week, I think that means you live here."

Tony looked at Carly. "How do you feel about that?"

"I love that you're here all the time. I want you to move in, I've just been waiting until I thought you were ready." Carly sat up on her knees and gripped Tony's face in her hands. Everyone watched, mesmerized by their love. "Anthony Scott, will you please move in with me and live with me always?"

He answered her with a kiss, one that went on and on. At least until Reed jumped on them.

"Hey," Ryan said, already standing to pull him off.

"It's okay," Carly said, pulling Reed into her side. "What do you think about that Reed? Tony living with us all the time?" She only called him Tony if she was talking to Reed. Otherwise it was always Anthony.

"He's there all the time."

Everyone in the room laughed. Even a six-year-old could tell that Tony had already been living there.

"I think that's our sign to pack it up and head out," Brandon said, standing and pulling Leah up with him.

One by one they left until it was only Addison and him. Carly had coaxed Reed into going back home with her and Tony, somehow knowing that he'd want the night alone with Addison.

In silence, they picked up the food and drinks, throwing them all in the trash. When everything was cleaned up, he leaned back against the counter and crossed his arms over his chest.

"Are you sure about this?"

She squinted her eyes at him in questioning. "About moving in? Yes. About me and you? Again, yes." She stepped toward him. "What do I have to do to convince you?"

He rubbed his chin with his thumb and index finger. "I have a few ideas, all of which I think you will like."

Her eyes glinted as she ran a hand through his hair. "I have no doubt that I will enjoy each and every one of your ideas." She stepped closer to him. "Why don't you show me?"

Reaching out, he used his arm to pull her close to him and, without a word, his mouth descended toward hers. He knew she was expecting fast and furious, but what he gave her instead, was slow and unhurried. He took his time, exploring every inch of her mouth. When he'd done all he could to her mouth, he moved down to her neck. He loved being able to feel her pulse with his lips.

"Remember that new bed that came just a little while ago?," she murmured.

He bit her neck softly. "We'll get there. Eventually." Spinning them so that her back was to the counter, he hauled her up onto it. Stepping between her widened legs, he kept up his assault on her neck.

Her hands began tearing at his clothing trying to get them off. He did the same, stripping off her shirt and then unsnapping her jeans and pulling them down her legs. While she kicked them off, he finished removing his own. It was hard to do when her hands and mouth were all over his chest taunting him. Stepping back between her legs, he pulled her so that her ass was right on the edge of the counter.

"You might need this." She was holding up a condom.

Grabbing it from her, he quickly opened it. Just when he was about to roll it on though, she spoke up.

"Let me."

Her hands reached between them and began to slowly roll it down his length.

"Addison," he huffed out, his hands gripping her hips. It felt so good to have her touch him. He didn't think he'd ever get tired of it.

Her hands finished and trailed up his chest and around his neck. Without words, because none were needed, he moved forward and entered her. He did it slowly to tease her, but all he ended up doing was torturing himself. Dropping his forehead to hers, he began to move. Later they would go slow, but for now, they both seemed to want the same thing.

Each other.

Moving in sync, they made love right there on the countertop, in their new kitchen. It was the perfect way to seal their love and christen their new home.

Also by Bree Kraemer

First Touch
Give & Go
Narrowing the Angle
He's A Keeper
Ground Rules
Walk Off
Sacrifice Bunt
Grand Slam (April 2023)

www.ingramcontent.com/pod-product-compliance
Lightning Source LLC
Chambersburg PA
CBHW051430130726
47987CB00005B/1992